The Entropy Heresy

The Entropy Heresy

Book Two of *The Heresy Series*

Jed Brody

Stormbird Press

Stormbird Press

Stormbird Press is an imprint
of Wild Migration Limited.

PO Box 73, Parndana, South Australia.
www.stormbirdpress.com

First published by Moon Willow Press, 2013.
Published by Stormbird Press, 2022.

Cover design by Júlia Both.
Typeset by Stormbird Press with Antique Olive and Kazimir.
Forest illustration by Potapov Alexander/Shutterstock.

National Library of Australia and State Library of South Australia
Legal Deposit
Brody, Jed, 1974—Author
The Entropy Heresy
ISBN 13: 978-1-925856-19-4 (pbk)
ISBN 13: 978-1-925856-20-0 (ebk)
1. Science Fiction | 2. Action & Adventure | 3. Dystopian | 4. Nature

*The publishing industry still pulps millions of books every year when
new titles fail to meet inflated sales projections—ploys designed to
saturate the market, crowding out other books.*

*This unacceptable practice creates tragic levels of waste. Paper
degrading in landfill releases methane—a greenhouse gas emission
23 times more potent than carbon dioxide.*

*Stormbird Press prints our books 'on demand', and from sustainable
forestry sources, to conserve Earth's precious, finite resources.*

We believe every printed book should find a home.

dedicated to the archangels

*Every blade of grass has its angel
that bends over it and whispers,
'Grow, grow.'*

–The Talmud

*Every wolf's and lion's howl raises
from Hell a human soul.*

–William Blake

Publisher's note

It's a breath-taking figure to contemplate. Nearly half of *Earth's* estimated 5.8 trillion trees cleared by humans. Grand old trees are falling fast.

Without trees, all hope seems lost, yet we continue to wipe these precious beings from the tropics for cattle, soybeans, and palm oil; from temperate regions by climate-driven wildfires; and from the planet's single largest biome—the boreal forests of Scandinavia to northern Canada through logging and ecosystem decline.

Most people understand we will struggle to survive in a world without trees, and yet, so many forests, that have stood for hundreds of years, now face extinction. These devastating losses should surely be mourned on a deep cultural level, enough to halt the terrible decline, and yet, we find ourselves in a space where brave, activist authors such as Jed Brody feel duty-bound to pen *The Heresy Series* as a siren call for the preservation and resurrection of the *Earth's* great forests.

Stormbird originally acquired Brody's dystopic series because his two brilliant books questioned, speculated and critiqued what our world would look like without trees. We embraced their underlying message and narrative brilliance, and imagined a future where humanity had failed to respond to deforestation in time.

We released Brody's *The Philodendrist Heresy* in 2019, and planned the release of the sequel, *The Entropy Heresy*, for early 2020. But then climate chaos wildfires razed our office, turned the surrounding fields to ash, and vaporised the ancient trees that had stretched their branches over us every day.

When people speak about wildfires, they often fail to grasp the scale of loss—not only to humans, but to the thousands of plants and animals, as well as coastal and river ecologies that once flourished downstream of fire zones.

Our entire ecosystem depended on trees, and it was in grave pain.

As the months crept along, we watched the blackened landscape struggle to survive without the living presence of its wise elders, now frail, charcoal skeletons. *The Heresy Series* came to have deeper, personal meaning to our team. Without huge eucalypts, graceful she-oaks, and charismatic banksia trees, our community became impoverished in ways we are only now beginning to understand. Forests affect people. When great trees burn or fall, we feel a life-changing wound to our soul.

Large, old trees are among the biggest organisms on *Earth*. They are keystone structures in forests, woodlands, savannas, and agricultural landscapes, playing unique ecological roles not provided by younger, smaller trees. Yet, populations of large, old trees are being annihilated throughout the world. This holds serious implications for ecosystem integrity and biodiversity—for humanity.

Let us hope, for all our sakes, that we heed Brody's warning, and that his work remains brilliant, compelling fiction, not prescience of times to come.

After all, even if we could live in a world without trees, who would want to?

Margi Prideaux
Publisher, Stormbird Press
November 30, 2021

1

You mustn't think, "Aladdin had a magic lamp; therefore, I need a magic lamp." You mustn't think, "Jack found a magic bean; therefore, I need a magic bean." If you chase after someone else's success, you will only meet with failure. If you follow your own unique dream, you will meet with success beyond imagining, though others may not recognize it as such.

–Janet Peptide, Sermon to the Empty Arena

Cougar did not move silently through the wooded hillside. Instead, he enhanced the sounds of the movement all around him. When the wind jostled the leaves and the grasses, he allowed his shoulders and feet to do the same. When a frog leapt from a stone into the stream, he allowed his toes to drag through a rivulet. Only when the forest was still did he move silently. And the forest was seldom still.

He broke no twigs and bent no stems. He feet touched down softly on stones or on existing depressions between fallen leaves. He left no trace of his passage, which required his movements to be precise, especially since he traveled at the pace of a brisk jog. Yet his attention was directed mostly to his surroundings: the salamanders scurrying to hide among the ferns, seemingly unaware that their tails protruded; the turtles mating lazily among the roots of an ancient sycamore; the cries of the crows mobbing a lone falcon far overhead.

His stealth was, perhaps, unnecessary at this time. He was far from the frontier with the brigand nation, and he was in no danger of ambush. The wolves in the area had recently gorged themselves on the migrating herds of elk and had no appetite for human meat. He, too, had hunted the elk with great success and had smoked ample meat for the coming winter; he had no immediate need to conceal his approach from any prey. Instead, as he often reminded Danielle Gasket, a hunter must always practice stealth, lest the people starve.

Cougar paused and rested his foot upon an oddly warm object. The object was round and hard, though its taut covering could be slid small distances from one side to the other. He grabbed a handful of pine needles and began to chew them.

"Cougar, get off my forehead," Danielle groaned. "And what have you been stepping in? Your feet smell even worse than usual."

"What marvel is this!" Cougar exclaimed. "The ground speaks! But no—it is an even greater wonder! A person, sleeping defenselessly out in the open, as though oblivious to the innumerable dangers!"

"You know better than I that I was in no danger," Danielle said. "The wolves have full bellies and never attack us anyway. The cougars and bears also don't attack us unless they feel threatened. And I've never even seen a brigand. I think you invented the brigand nation just to scare me. And seriously about your foot. It stinks. Get it off my head."

"Unless you imagine that great peril surrounds you every instant, it will catch you unprepared when it inevitably arrives," Cougar said. "You could at least have camouflaged yourself with ash and mud."

"We hunted elk all night, and I was tired," Danielle said. "Why do you always work me so hard? You made me survive all alone last winter, after I'd been out of the crypt nation only a few months. Isn't my training over yet?"

"You don't even have the skills of a brigand," Cougar said. "You wouldn't survive a week in the brigand nation, which, you know, will be the test at the end of your training. How many squirrels are currently on the red oak to your left? How many starling eggs are in the nest on the highest branch? What's the favorite food of the box turtle in the closest pond? You don't know any these things, and you don't even know how I know. You don't even know why they're important."

"Yes, I do," Danielle said, slamming her hand into the back of Cougar's knee and hurling him forward. "I need to know the turtle's favorite food, for example, in order to use the proper bait."

Cougar landed in a defensive crouch, and Danielle tackled empty air as he leapt out of the way. Danielle sprang off the ground with her hands, driving her heels into Cougar's throat just as he seized her neck with his fingers. They collapsed into a groaning heap.

"You're getting a lot better at that," Cougar said after catching his breath. His face was somehow wedged between Danielle's kneecap and armpit.

"I have a good teacher," Danielle said. She slid her fingers from Cougar's bald head to his thick, black beard. "But can't my training continue after I get some more rest? I couldn't have slept more than two hours."

"Chrysalis just received troubling news from the cherub nation," Cougar said. "There's some kind of emergency. She's with Jaguar and Panther. They're waiting for us. We'd assemble more people, but there's no time. We need to go. Now."

His lips briefly brushed Danielle's as he helped her to her feet, and they ran together through the wooded hillside, leaving no trace, and making no sounds except for those of their surroundings.

2

People call me misanthropic, but I hate
them for that.
–Janet Peptide, I Laugh To Keep from Belching

Few indeed perished while testing their skills in the brigand nation; the free nation forbade its warriors to test until their survival was all but assured. Cougar, though uncommonly stalwart, had come closer to death than most.

Morel's knife should have pierced Cougar's heart. Instead, as Cougar vaulted backwards over a log and into a ten-foot-deep ravine, the knife tip slashed from his clavicle to his hip—a long wound, but not a deep one.

Morel leapt after him, and with a small stone he deflected her knife thrusts. His blood glistened wetly in the afternoon sunlight.

"How can it be that you parry so swiftly?" Morel demanded. "Six men have I slain after harvesting their seed. Surely no man can battle as skillfully as you."

"No brigand man possesses skills such as mine," Cougar panted, "but I am no brigand. I am a warrior of the free nation."

Morel's eyes widened in wonder, and she doubled the speed of her attack.

"So you are not from this land of conquerors at all!" she spat. "You are from the land of cowards!"

"I suppose that's what you call us," Cougar said.

He tripped Morel but waited passively until she rose and renewed her assault.

"You have just proven your cowardice!" Morel taunted. "A true conqueror would have slain me then."

"And yet, you cannot best me," Cougar said.

"This is true," Morel said. "Never in the history of my sisterhood has a man survived the harvest. This can only mean that our daughter will be a great and fearsome warrior. She will push outward our borders! She will rise against your people! All will fall to her spear!"

"Explain yourself," Cougar said. "How do you know that it won't be a son?"

"In my sisterhood, all boys must be slain," Morel said. "It has been my curse to bear six sons. But now you have lifted my curse! You have given me the greatest daughter of all, the bane of your own nation!"

"I don't believe you," Cougar said. "Your boasts are hollow. Your threat is imagined."

"Then why is your fear real?" Morel sneered.

She threw down her knife.

"If you are not a coward, then prove it!" she shouted. "Slay me now and save your people! Or spare me, and herald their ruin!"

Cougar grimaced and picked up the knife. Morel raised her chin and began to laugh.

"I pity the sorrow you bring upon yourself through your misguided mercy toward me," she said.

She felt the knife tip against her throat, and she closed her eyes.

"Or was I wrong?" she asked.

When she opened her eyes, she was alone in the ravine, and her laughter rang out into the forest.

3

Like all too many wonders of nature, wind is fragile. I break it often.

–Janet Peptide, I Laugh To Keep from Belching

"Wait!" Danielle gasped, braking hard against a poplar trunk. "Stop!"

Cougar halted, and Danielle crouched low. She examined a thin, braided cord concealed among tall grasses.

"It's a trap!" Danielle said. She drew a stone knife from the sheath on her belt, and she quickly disarmed the trap. She and Cougar hurried ahead, and they came upon a mossy boulder at the edge of a gurgling stream. Chrysalis and Jaguar were sitting upon the boulder. Jaguar rubbed his hands over his short, tightly coiled hair, which was black with gray patches.

"You're doing a good job with her, brother," Jaguar said. "She's learning fast." He did not smile, but his voice was warm. Chrysalis, however, folded her arms and stared coldly at Danielle.

"Where's Panther?" Danielle asked.

"Guess I spoke too soon," Jaguar grunted.

Chrysalis sighed, and her red dreadlocks shifted on her shoulders. Panther dropped down from an overhanging branch. His thin, black braids bounced briefly.

"Oh, I forgot to look up," Danielle said. "Sorry." She looked at the ground, trying to pay attention to the beetles and decaying leaves, but instead felt her cheeks flush with embarrassment and anger.

Panther smiled and embraced her.

"Don't let them get you down," he said. "We're all amazed how much you've learned in just one year. The feigned disappointment is part of the training. We all went through it as children."

Panther squeezed Danielle arms.

"Really?" Danielle said, hastily brushing her fingers across her eyes.

"Yes," Panther said with a grin. "Though now that I've given away our secret, I'll be taken behind a boulder and garroted. We do have some barbaric customs that you don't know about yet."

Danielle and Cougar laughed, but Chrysalis slapped the stone.

"We don't have time for this," Chrysalis snapped. "We are in grave danger, and our peril is linked to you, Danielle Gasket of the crypt nation."

"What? How?" Danielle said. "What did I do?"

"Your ascent from the crypt nation has had repercussions," Chrysalis said. "The old equilibrium is collapsing. The brigands are emboldened. A new power has arrived on the coasts. We do not know what the future holds. We must only fight to survive day to day."

"What are you talking about?" Danielle said. "How have I emboldened the brigands? How do they even know I'm here?"

"Why don't you explain that to us, crypt-born witch!" Chrysalis said. "What foul sorceries do you employ to commune with your murderous brethren?"

"You've made your suspicions clear," Cougar said. "Just tell us what you heard from the cherub nation."

Chrysalis bared her teeth and shivered with fury. "How you defend the crypt-born witch! You used to prefer women of the free nation."

Cougar looked away uncomfortably.

"The old equilibrium has already collapsed," Panther said gently, "on every scale, from large to small. If our hearts are embittered by this, then we poison every effort we make. We cannot establish a new, harmonious equilibrium when disharmony reigns in our hearts."

"The old equilibrium was harmonious," Chrysalis said, glaring at Cougar. "It is not too late to reestablish it. But listen to what has befallen.

"A large number of brigands recently sought refuge in the cherub nation. The brigands swore they sought only to escape daily bloodshed and cruelty. They asked to be trained in the ways of the cherub nation. This is nothing new. We, too, have welcomed repentant brigands into our nation. We monitor them closely until they have proven their loyalty to our ways. They often astound us with their generosity. They seem sincerely compelled to atone.

"And yet, now, the cherub nation reports that the new brigands had deceived them. These brigands slaughtered entire settlements and plundered their supplies."

"This shows the carelessness of the cherub nation," Jaguar snorted. "This shows how addled their minds become from want of meat."

"Nay, brother," Panther said. "When I lived in the cherub nation, I found them to be masters of reading hidden intentions from people's faces. They can even divine people's intentions from their footprints! Here in the free nation, we have none who match them at this skill, though I tried my best to learn it.

"If the brigands succeeded in deceiving the

cherub nation, then some new witchery must truly have been employed. The people of the cherub nation are not only unsurpassed at reading intentions; they are also the fiercest warriors I have met. It is true that they never hunt game, but they practice ceaselessly with lifeless targets. I believe that their unvented bloodlust makes them more ferocious than any of our own warriors."

"Which makes the following news even more unsettling," Chrysalis said. "For the first time in untold generations, a vessel appeared on the great waters lapping the beaches of the cherub nation. As the vessel approached the shore, the warriors of the cherub nation gathered with bows and spears.

"The vessel anchored a short distance from the shore, and a woman dived from the vessel into the sea. Thinking this some new trick of the brigands, the warriors aimed their arrows. The woman from the vessel swam swiftly towards them. She stood when the water came only to her thighs. She wore a gown of seaweed, and shells were braided into her hair."

"That sounds like a dream you once spoke of, Cougar," Panther said.

"Aye, brother," Cougar said. "When I was fourteen, I sometimes had that dream three times a night."

Chrysalis narrowed her eyes. "Will you try to

say focused on what I'm saying?"

"Oh, I'm focused," Cougar said. "Could you go back to the part about the seaweed gown? Was it the thick, black seaweed, or the green, translucent kind? And how loosely was it woven?"

"Somehow, the emissaries of the cherub nation, fearing for the lives of their kin, neglected to fill in those details," Chrysalis said. "Can I resume? Now listen. The warriors ordered the woman to halt, but she continued to approach. Reluctantly, the warriors loosed their arrows, but the woman dodged or deflected them all! Then the warriors lunged at her with their spears, but she kicked water into their eyes, and in that instant, the warriors felt their spears wrested from their hands. When they opened their eyes, their spears were nowhere to be seen.

"'Who are you!' the warriors cried. 'Why have you come upon us?'

"The woman answered, 'These questions would have been a more courteous welcome, rather than arrows and spears, no? But no matter. I come from the sea nation. We guard the deadly canisters of poisons that were buried on islands before the time of the interment. The canisters have begun to leak, as we knew they would; as their designers knew they would. Some fish and marsh grasses have already begun to show signs of poisoning. We need to heal them, and the only cure is the elixir of the crypt nation; the antidote to the devil's venom comes only from the devil. Hurry back with the elixir. We have little time. Unchecked, the sickness will soon spread, and the angels will twist in dying torment, and the archangels will rot like fruit, and none will remain to hold even the remembrance of life.'

"Still unsure whether to trust this woman, the warriors sent messengers to us. Word of Danielle's ascent had already reached the cherub nation. Perhaps Danielle herself is the elixir, and we must deliver her to them."

"I'm no elixir," Danielle said, "and I've never even heard of it, but I know of crypt-born specialists who build machines. They call themselves technicians. Maybe they've built some kind of elixir machine. I can go looking for it. I never wanted to return to the crypt nation, but it's clear that I have to."

"You'll descend into the crypt, and return with a barbarian army!" Chrysalis said. "It's too dangerous to let you down there, now that you know our secrets. Tell us what we must do, and we will go."

"But you have no idea how anything works down there!" Danielle said. "It's more complicated than you can imagine. Even if time were not a factor, I'd never be able to arm you with every necessary fact; there are just too many details. You don't even know how to find food and water. You don't even know how to find a bathroom!"

"What's a bathroom?" Cougar said.

"Oh, wow," Danielle said. "See? It's even worse than I'd thought. I'm getting a better appreciation of your patience with me over the past year."

"It's true, Chrysalis," Jaguar said. "Danielle needs to be part of this. But we'll accompany her."

"But there's room in the vehicle for only three people, maybe four," Danielle said.

"What's a vehicle?" Panther asked.

"Sorry," Danielle said. "It's a machine that moves you around, much faster than you can walk or even run. I rode the vehicle a very great distance from the crypt nation."

"How long would it take to run that distance?" Cougar asked. "So that more than four people can go."

"I'm really not sure," Danielle said. "Most of the time I was asleep. Or in a trance. Or maybe some kind of a stupor. I'm not sure which. Anyway, I'd guess it would take at least a week to run the distance, and that's if you take little time to rest or sleep."

"A week is too long," Chrysalis said. "We must ride the vehicle. Cougar will stay behind because his basest appetites tend to cloud his better judgment."

"There's nothing wrong with Cougar's appetites at present," Danielle said, "though they may have been questionably whetted in the past."

"We can't let this petty quarrel interfere

with a mission of such importance!" Jaguar growled. "Danielle has to be a part of this, and Chrysalis, your hostility toward her, however understandable, is just too much of a liability. You're the one who has to stay behind."

Panther nodded. Chrysalis looked slowly from Panther, to Cougar, and then to Danielle. Several sparrows chirped unseen among the branches, and two squirrels chased each other around the trunk of elm.

"If this is your decision, then I accept it," Chrysalis said. "Just remember the words of the woman from the sea nation. Someone with power like hers does not speak lightly. An ancient venom is seeping into our waters. You must address this evil with the greatest possible urgency."

"After the sun has moved two fingers through the sky, we'll meet at the lake where Danielle ascended," Jaguar said. "Take bows, arrows, knives, and stones. Take tinder and spindles to make fire. Take food and water. Everything in the crypt nation is poison."

"Crypt-born," Chrysalis said. "I would have a word with you." Her dreadlocks hung over her face.

Danielle waited until the others departed. "Yes?"

"You have amazed us, truly, with your rapid mastery of the arts of stealth and combat. You can more than take care of yourself. So I ask you to keep an eye on Cougar. His excessive confidence is his vulnerability. Take good care of him, will you?"

"I—I will," Danielle said. She tried to see Chrysalis's eyes through the red dreadlocks, but she could not. Once or twice, Chrysalis's shoulders seemed to shake, and hearing no further instructions, Danielle departed.

Cougar watched from an overhanging branch as Chrysalis wept. For the first time in his life, Cougar did not know what to do, and he crouched silently until Chrysalis, too, departed.

"Have you no preparations to make, brother?" Panther asked from a higher branch.

"How did you find me?" Cougar said.

"I followed your tracks, of course," Panther said. "I may have stopped hunting, but I haven't stopped tracking. Remember, I'm almost as good at tracking as you are."

"But I leave no tracks," Cougar said.

"Not usually," Panther said. "Only once every forty or fifty paces. You're getting a little careless. And tell me, brother, where is your tinder pouch?"

"Right here on my belt, of course—" Cougar said, but then he gasped.

"Or is it here in my hand?" Panther said. "How careless have you become? It is prudent to exercise all our skills to the fullest as we prepare to descend into enemy nations."

"That seems wise, brother," Cougar said. "I am

certain that our skills in stealth and tracking will make us invulnerable among the crypt-born."

"Then why do you frown at the sky?"

"Moments ago, I saw four bats fly by, which is odd, in the middle of the day," Cougar said. "Then only two returned."

Panther shrugged. "It means nothing."

"But the strangest thing," Cougar said, "is that only one of the four original bats returned. The other bat was new."

"It means nothing," Panther repeated. "Now come, we must prepare to depart."

Cougar continued to frown at the sky, and Panther descended the tree alone. He bent near the earth and then dashed silently forward, following another set of tracks. He stopped some distance from Jaguar, who sat on rocks near a stream. Jaguar was muttering to himself, indecipherably at first, but then with crisp articulation.

"Mother," Jaguar said, staring at the flowing water, "I never thought I would go on without you. I thought I would rest forever in your embrace. But now, full of your nourishment, I must leave you, and seek my own fortune. I take along all you have given me. I stand upon all you have taught me. My success is your success, and my failure is also your success, for you have taught me that none can escape the blessed fruition of destiny. Let my heart drum out a song of love for you, and when the drum at last goes silent, I will return to you, forever."

Panther silently departed, ducking under low branches and stepping over tall reeds. Crypt-born Danielle Gasket, who also watched Jaguar from the shadows, wondered if the brothers only pretended not to see her.

4

Is it just me, or is there a self-deprecating
misfit at this party?

–Janet Peptide, I Laugh To Keep from Belching

Derek Gasket lay on the floor and sniffled. He held a crayon in his fist and stared at a blank piece of paper.

"Derek! What's wrong?" Danielle asked, skipping into the room while jumping rope. "Daddy says I can't go listen to the clarinets until I cheer you up. He's given up, he says. Why are you sad?"

"I still don't know my letters," Derek said.

"You already know how to write, and you're two years younger than me. Mommy and Daddy are frustrated with me. Even Tommy said he's losing patience with me, and he's never mean to anyone."

"Well, that's not your fault," Danielle said. She dropped the jump rope and began bouncing a yellow rubber ball. "Any time anyone can't learn anything, it's the teacher's fault."

"Really?" Derek said, scrambling into a seated position.

"Of course," Danielle said. "I read that somewhere."

"Where?" Derek said.

"On the piece of paper I'd just written it on!"

Derek giggled.

"Are there any letters that are easier for you than others?" Danielle asked.

"Yeah," Derek said. "I'm better with letters that look the same way forwards and backwards, like H, or W. I have trouble with letters that are wrong to flip around, like S. Especially S. I write it both ways, but I can never remember which is right."

"Well, I have an idea," Danielle said. "Why don't you trace the letters that I write? Don't think about how the letters look. Think about how it feels in your hand when you write them correctly. Maybe it will be easier to remember with your hand than your head."

"You think that will work?" Derek said. He tapped his head with his crayon.

"I don't know, so we have to try to find out," Danielle said.

Derek frowned. "But if I trace your letters, then I'll write like a girl!"

"Not at all!" Danielle said. "Because everyone says I write like boy!"

"Really?" Derek said, brightening.

"Really," Danielle said. "Now let's start with that S."

5

When the dark spring breezes spill out of the east, and the sun-lent warmth rises like spirits from the stones, I gaze up at the black silhouettes of the trees against the night sky. Then I feel the love that surpasses human love, and I dissolve into the Divine Mother's embrace. And every time I enter a building, I feel that I am leaving Eden, and every time I return outside, I fear that Eden won't be there anymore. These are the central experiences of my life.

–Janet Peptide, Sermon to the Empty Arena

Danielle stood bald at the edge of the lake.

"Is everyone bald in the crypt nation?" Panther

said nervously, stroking his braids.

"No," Danielle said. "I just don't want any of my old enemies to recognize me. I'll need to wrap something around my face."

"You haven't seen yourself change over the past year," Cougar said, "but we have. Emerging from the crypt nation, you were skeletal. Pallid. I've seen healthier complexions on dead people. You're unrecognizable now."

"Really?" Danielle said.

Cougar nodded and knelt to fill a waterskin in the lake.

"Do you all have everything you need?" Jaguar asked. He adjusted his bow, quiver, and pouches, and everyone nodded. "Then take the lead, Danielle."

"Somewhere in the middle of the lake, toward the northeast, there's a submerged wall with the opening to an underwater tunnel," Danielle said. "We have to swim through the tunnel into a room. Do you even know what a room is? It's surrounded by walls and a ceiling, which is a solid surface over your head. The vehicle wouldn't fit through the tunnel, so I left it in that room. Let's go."

She waded into the lake and began to swim as the others followed. Geese and ducks squawked and splashed out of their way. Danielle savored the taste of the pure water on her lips, and she remembered the stale, dusty flavor of the water in the crypt nation.

"Here it is," Cougar said, surfacing to the left. Water dribbled down his head, his bow, and his other burdens. "I'll go first and make sure it's safe. Wait here."

"Cougar, there's no need for chivalry—" Danielle said, but Cougar was gone.

Panther playfully splashed Danielle, and she tugged his braids, while Jaguar shook his head irritably. Cougar rose again from the water.

"No one's been in that room for a year," Cougar said. "The only tracks are Danielle's."

Danielle and the three brothers inhaled deeply and swam through the tunnel. They stepped out into a pool in a square room. A sleek vehicle with a large, open hatch emitted white light from an interior panel. A cavernous tunnel led from the wall opposite the pool.

"Great fires!" Jaguar gagged, dripping water. "I hope the air gets better deeper in the crypt nation."

"Oh, no," Danielle said. "It only gets worse. The air right here is almost as good as the air outside. It gets much, much worse."

Jaguar groaned and shook his head. "The crypt-born are much tougher than I'd thought. I'd die after a few days of the air right here. It smells like an opossum carcass embalmed with skunk urine."

"What's that?" Panther asked, pointing at a rectangular object on the seat of the vehicle. The object had ten buttons labeled 0 through 9.

"That's a transmitter," Danielle said. "Try not to get it too wet. It might break. It's an indispensable survival tool in the crypt nation. It controls the machines. Most crypt-born have never even heard of transmitters. But I have powerful enemies, so I need powerful tools."

"How does it work?" Cougar asked.

"What are those symbols on it?" Jaguar said.

"You have so much to learn!" Danielle said. "I'll teach you as we ride. It'll be fun to be the teacher, for once. Let's get in. It'll be a tight squeeze. Maybe we can stow our bows, quivers, and waterskins in front of our feet, like this."

They loaded their equipment into the vehicle. Danielle sat down first. She took the transmitter and stored it in her driest pocket. She slid in so that Cougar could sit next to her. Panther slid in from the other side, and finally Jaguar followed Panther. Safety belts began to slide around their waists, but the three brothers severed them with stone knives before Danielle could explain that they were harmless. Danielle dripped uncomfortably.

"How long is this ride going to be?" Jaguar grumbled. "I feel like a toad in a snake's throat."

"I think about seven hours, judging by how refreshed I felt after sleeping through the ride up," Danielle said. "We should sleep on our way down, but only after I finish teaching you the essentials of life in the crypt nation."

"Seven hours in a snake's throat," Jaguar sighed. "And the snake is saying really boring things."

"The crypt nation is anything but boring!" Danielle said. "I think it's going to be a fun place to visit, considering we're bringing our own food and water. The crypt-born don't have to hunt or forage or make clothing or shelter. Everything is provided by the machines. So people spend their entire lives pursuing their hobbies: art, music, athletics, literature. But I'm getting ahead of myself. Let's start moving. Hatch, close."

The hatch closed, sealing them in the vehicle. Jaguar, Panther, and Cougar had all drawn their knives and were aiming them at the hatch. Danielle laughed.

"I asked the vehicle to do that, silly boys!" Danielle said. "Some machines respond to vocal commands. Like this: return me to where I first got in."

The vehicle wheeled around and entered the large tunnel.

"This machine understands language?" Cougar said.

"It's alive?" Panther said.

"It understands language, but it's not alive," Danielle said. "It doesn't think. It doesn't make decisions. Its behavior is perfectly predicable, except for when it breaks down, which happens all too often with most machines. There are machines that repair or replace broken machines. I'm not sure which machines repair the machines that repair other machines. Maybe they all repair one another. Or maybe all the machines are slowly disintegrating, and some day there will be no more food or water. Nobody likes to talk about this. Those few who do talk about it call it the entropy heresy. People are scared, and they're scared to admit why they're scared. They're scared of unseen forces that make bad things happen to people who question the way things are.

"The dominant unseen force is the warden. Most people don't know about him explicitly, but they fear that someone like him exists. He entices or bullies a lot of people into working for him. These people have guns, which launch small, deadly stones so fast that you can't see them. You're quick, but even you can't outmaneuver these stones. And if you see a gun, it's probably best not to take it, as long as you still have arrows. Sometimes guns misfire, and you could maim yourself.

"Most people are harmless, even frail. They live in complete ignorance of the heaven we just left. They pursue their hobbies all their lives, and then they die. Some people, however, are very dangerous. They have partial knowledge of heaven, and they seek to travel, control, or destroy the tunnel we now occupy. You can't trust anyone. You mustn't do anything unusual that would attract the attention of hostile elements. So you need to know what's normal and what's not."

"We're really not as helpless as you think," Cougar said, wedged between Danielle and the side of the vehicle. "There is much we have yet to teach you about tracking. We can tell from people's tracks how long it's been since they've eaten. The tracks change when their weight changes. Similarly, we can figure out where people perform other necessary functions."

"Oh," Danielle said. "Still, you need to understand the words people use to describe the places where they do these things. A restaurant is a place where they eat. A bathroom is a place where something else happens."

"The very concept makes me gag," Jaguar said.

"You'll figure it out," Danielle laughed. "It's not as disgusting as you think. Now, a warehouse is a place where you can find clothes, tools, chairs, and anything else that anyone has in the crypt nation. You just take whatever you want. You don't have to barter or anything. The machines keep the warehouses supplied.

"A library is a place with books. Oh no! You don't know how to read! You really would be helpless without me. Well, don't worry about it. Just protect me well, and I'll read whatever needs reading.

"You also need to know about vehicles. The vehicle we're riding is special, but most vehicles come in four varieties: maintenance vehicles, medic vehicles, taxis, and leisure carriages. The maintenance vehicles are the machines that repair things. The medic vehicles repair people, but you're probably better off repairing yourselves. Taxis take you to specific destinations. And leisure carriages seek to maximize the pleasure registered in your brain.

"This transmitter controls vehicles and other machines, even those that don't respond to vocal commands. These symbols represent numbers. To get machines to obey the commands, you first have to type the identification number of the machine, and then you have to type the four-digit number representing the command. Out of respect for the traditions of the technicians' guild, I never wrote down the commands I learned; I had to memorize them. It's really hard to do, and since we only have one transmitter, I'll handle this. But you should know that if two transmitters try to get the same machine to do different things, the conflict is resolved by a hierarchy. Every transmitter occupies a certain position in the hierarchy. I don't know where this one lies, but the warden's transmitter is at the top of the hierarchy.

"Finally, you need to understand the layout of the crypt nation. The smallest unit is called a block. It's about a thousand paces long in every direction. One block can contain many buildings. If you get 1000 blocks and arrange them in a cube, ten by ten by ten, you have a precinct. If you get an incalculable number of precincts and arrange them in a cube, 201 by 201 by 201, you have the crypt nation. So the total number of blocks is staggering."

"Then however will we find the elixir?" Cougar said.

"I once heard a technician mention a big project in the B4D block of precinct $x = -0.10$, $y = 0.37$, $z = -0.29$, so that's where we'll look first," Danielle said. "And since you're so resourceful, maybe you can figure out how the blocks are named."

"Is there anything else we really have to know?" Jaguar asked gruffly. "I think we should try to sleep."

"I think that's all for now," Danielle said.

Jaguar closed his eyes.

"You know why I'm so excited to journey to crypt nation?" Panther whispered. "In the cherub nation, I learned a little of the art of telepathy. My efforts were unsuccessful when I tried to read the thoughts of my instructors. But I soon discovered another person's thoughts within my awareness, and he detected mine! As we conversed in this way, I discovered, to my astonishment, that he dwelt in the crypt nation! I have told him I am coming. I hope that we may meet."

"And that, Danielle," Jaguar said, eyes still

closed, "is the sort of mad delusion people fall prey to when they stop eating meat."

Panther shrugged and winked at Danielle.

"Tell me more of the cherub nation," Danielle said.

"Quietly," Cougar added, closing his eyes and nuzzling Danielle's bald scalp.

"One legend in the cherub nation is that just before you die, you hear the cries of gulls, and your saliva thickens and tastes like honey," Panther said. "And then there's the tale of—"

Danielle snored softly upon Cougar's shoulder. Panther smiled, but he looked away, and he wiped a tear from his eye.

6

*Something keeps biting me in my sleep,
again and again on my lower legs. The doctor
discovered, to my horror, that the tooth marks were
my own.*

–Janet Peptide, I Laugh To Keep from Belching

"Mommy! Where's my favorite shirt!" Danielle shouted. "The purple one with green pockets!"

"I'm patching up the elbows for you," her mother called from the next room. "Again."

Danielle sighed and trotted into the other room. "But it's my birthday. I want to wear my favorite shirt."

Her mother sat on a soft chair covered by a

brown blanket with pink polka dots.

"Well, you'll just have to wait, Danielle."

Danielle shifted her weight from foot to foot. "I shouldn't have to wait on my birthday."

"What's your hurry?" her mother asked. "What are you so impatient to do?"

"There are really tall columns on the bottom floor of the music library," Danielle said. "I want to go climb them."

"All by yourself?"

Danielle nodded.

"Don't you want to bring a friend?" her mother asked. "How about your brother?"

"Derek smells," Danielle said.

"Danielle, that's not nice!"

"No, it's not," Danielle said. "He should bathe once in a while."

Her mother sighed. "You know that's not what I meant. I'm sorry there aren't more children your age on this block. I keep telling your father we should move to another block, but he's afraid of breaking his vase collection."

Danielle shrugged. "I'm happy here. I'm happy by myself. I don't want to wait for my favorite shirt. Can I go climb the columns now?"

"Okay, but make sure you eat first."

Danielle stuck out her tongue and held her stomach. "Do I really have to eat on my birthday?"

"Yes, Danielle, you have to eat every day. I'm sorry it hurts your stomach so much. I wish I could make it feel better. Just try not to think about it, okay?"

"Okay," Danielle said.

"Make sure you're back here within an hour so that we can sing to you."

"Three hours," Danielle said.

"One hour," her mother repeated.

"Two hours," Danielle said.

"Four hours, starting three hours ago."

Danielle leaned her head to one side. "That's still one hour!"

Her mother smiled. "You're so clever, Danielle. If you're having a really good time climbing the columns, you can stay two hours."

"Hooray!" Danielle shouted, running to give her mother a hug. Then Danielle ran out the door.

"Don't forget to eat!" her mother called after her.

Danielle ran down the street, ignoring the taxis, leisure carriages, and street performers. She slowed near the restaurant, eying it suspiciously. She decided to eat after climbing because it was hard to climb a column with a stomachache. She ran as fast as she could through an intersection, and then she turned left at the next street. She elbowed her way through a thicket of people practicing headstands. Half of them toppled over.

"Oops! Sorry!" she giggled, and then she entered the music library.

She ran among the cluttered shelves, leaping

over stacks of papers and books. She climbed over a railing positioned in the middle of an aisle. She stopped and caught her breath when she reached a cluster of thick columns. They were decorated with wide ribbons and splashes of bright paint. Danielle did not know why the columns were here since they did not even reach all the way to the luminous ceiling.

One of the columns was covered with knobs, which made it easy to climb. Danielle had already mastered that one. She now approached a perfectly smooth column. She held it between her hands and tried to walk up it with her feet, but her hands slipped. Then she squeezed her arms around the column, pressing it tightly against her chest. She raised one foot off the ground, then the other. She was able to hold herself up with her arms. She wrapped her legs around the column, pressed downward with her feet, and slid slightly upward.

She repeated this action several times, but only succeeded in raising herself a few feet off the ground. Frustrated, she leaned to one side, flailing her legs in search of a better grip. A deep, popping sound came from her lower ribcage, where her weight was braced against the column. Suddenly, she was unable to breathe. She dropped to the ground and lay on her side.

She tried to gasp, but a sharp pain ripped through her side. Her vision began to cloud, and she felt dizzy. She wondered if she were dying. She forced herself to take a small sip of air. The pain in her side felt like serrated knives, but she took another sip. Then she let out the air as a brief wheeze, which further rattled her ribs. Continuing to take deliberate, painful sips, she was able to keep from fainting.

She tried to shift into a seated position, but the movement intensified the pain in her side. Then she held herself as still as possible and devoted all her effort to breathing. After more than an hour, she was able to sit up. Slowly, gasping and holding her side, she began to limp away from the columns.

Back in her apartment, her mother was happy for her. Since Danielle hadn't returned yet, after more than an hour, she was presumably having a very nice time climbing.

7

Life is like a porcelain vase falling in the dark. You never know when it's going to strike the ground and shatter.

–Janet Peptide, Epistle from the Asylum

Danielle blinked her eyes open as the vehicle slowed. By the light from the vehicle's panel, she dimly saw a closed door blocking the tunnel ahead. Looking from side to side, she saw that Cougar and Panther were already awake, though Jaguar's eyes were still closed.

"Should we wake him up?" Danielle whispered. "I'm going to open the door with the transmitter. I want to show you how it works, just in case you need to use it."

"Rouse him at your own risk," Cougar said.

"Sometimes he's ornery when he wakes."

"And other times, he's merely flatulent," Panther added.

"I am awake," Jaguar growled. "I'm listening. I hear a low rumble like distant thunder, though there are patterns that repeat themselves."

"Those are probably the pumps that circulate air, water, food, and waste through the crypt nation," Danielle said. "I never noticed it before."

She aimed her transmitter at the door.

"You see those symbols on the door?" she said. "That's the identification number for the door. I type that into the transmitter. Then I want the door to open, so I type 7361, which is the code that means 'open.'"

The door opened with a creak, revealing an icy pool from which white mist rose.

"That water's so cold that if you jump in with clothes on, your clothes freeze solid, and you drown," Danielle said. "I'm a little afraid of what the water will do to this vehicle. It seems identical to a vehicle I saw on the other side of the pool, and that vehicle was apparently designed to withstand this water. I think these vehicles are made of a special material resistant to cold. But to be safe, let's get out and see what happens when the vehicle enters the pool."

The hatch opened at Danielle's command, and they climbed out of the vehicle. She tapped on the transmitter, and the hatch closed, and the vehicle rolled into the water. The water churned and hissed as the vehicle submerged, but it appeared undamaged. Then the vehicle rose and sputtered back onto the floor. Thin wisps of mist rose all around it. Cougar touched the hatch but quickly withdrew his hand.

"I've never felt anything so cold!" he said. "It burns!"

Danielle commanded the hatch to open, and they all peered inside. The interior remained dry and relatively warm. Cougar leapt inside the vehicle without touching the exterior, and the rest of them followed. Danielle typed additional commands. The hatch closed, and the vehicle trundled into the pool.

"Crypt nation," Jaguar said, "we come in peace."

The vehicle began its descent, and Danielle slid her hand into Cougar's. Large bubbles formed and jittered on the outer surface the window. They descended about forty feet and came to a submerged opening in the wall ahead of them. A faint blue glow shimmered through the opening. The vehicle swayed and then traversed the opening.

"We just crossed the only known passageway into the crypt nation," Danielle said.

The vehicle now rose, and the light through the window intensified, even as the bubbles grew, burst, and reformed. Finally, the vehicle broke through floating chunks of ice and maneuvered toward the edge of the pool. It lurched onto solid ground.

"Welcome to my homeland," Danielle said. "Open."

The hatch opened, and Jaguar retched.

"You cannot expect me to believe that you breathed air this putrescent all your life," he spat.

"Actually, you're right," Danielle said. "This block has some kind of sewage facility, so it's particularly bad." She coughed, feeling an old sting in her throat. "Though it's worse than I remembered."

She stood on the seat and leaped out of the vehicle. She looked around as her companions followed her. At the edge of the pool was a rumpled pile of her old clothes. The vehicle that she had disabled faced her from the center of the room. The putrefied remains of Roger Clade, her friend and former enemy, lay next to the vehicle.

Cougar crept around the room in a low crouch. His bow and quiver were already on his back. "No one has been is this room for a year," he said. "There's dust and grime all over the floor. This is almost as easy as tracking in sand.

"That dead man entered the room with Danielle. Then seven others entered. One of the seven was their leader. The others looked to him deferentially. The six subordinates each launched some kind of projectile at the dead man; I can see how they rocked back on their heels."

Cougar squinted and frowned, lowering his face closer to the ground.

"There was some kind of a confusion. Almost a scuffle. No, they suddenly stumbled blindly into one other, as though they were no longer able to see. The leader launched five projectiles in a variety of directions, and then he departed with his men. We can follow them easily, if we wish."

"Their leader is the warden," Danielle said. "He's very cunning. Even if we decided to track him down, it would be riskier than you think to subdue him. And even if we succeeded, I think that another warden would arise to take his place."

Panther walked delicately among the tracks, which were so faint that Danielle could scarcely see them.

"The warden bears his weight on the outer edges of his feet, somewhat toward the toes," Panther said. "His big toes never touch the ground. This shows a severe physical disorder. He suffers terrible pain near the floor of his trunk. That which brings others pleasure, brings him pain. Even walking is sometimes an ordeal for him. The impact with the ground feels jarring. He has to wear very soft shoes."

Cougar frowned at the ground. "I don't see any of that," he said.

Panther smiled. "I learned how to do this in the cherub nation."

"I see," Cougar said, glancing at Danielle with

raised eyebrows. "Then those conclusions are suspect."

Panther shook his head and sighed. "I know the herb that would cure the warden, or at least mitigate his pains. It's a pity I don't have it here. If only I had time to go back for it."

"You would heal our enemy?" Jaguar said, looking up from the ground.

"His suffering is the root of his villainy," Panther said. "He could become a potent ally if I healed him."

Danielle marveled at his words, and Jaguar strode over to Roger's corpse.

"This man died of multiple wounds to the abdomen," he said. "He had previously sustained many other injuries, some recently, some not. His right thigh had been shattered and was expertly set. A number of his teeth are prosthetic, and so is one of his toes. His ribs deflected at least three knives."

Danielle shook her head.

"I was so proud of how much I learned over the past year," she said. "But I still have so much more to learn from you."

"It'll be something to look forward to," Cougar said. "Besides, we should hurry onward instead of satisfying our curiosity about what transpired in this room. What do we do now?"

"I think I should hide the amphibious vehicle on the other side of the pool," Danielle said. "It could attract too much attention if we ride it, and I don't think it's safe to leave it here. Even though no one's been here for a year, our arrival could trigger some kind of alarm."

Jaguar nodded. "But how will you get back to this side of the pool?"

"I'll swim," Danielle said. "That's how I made it through the pool the first time."

"That's too dangerous for you," Cougar said. "I'll do it. You stay here."

Jaguar dipped a finger in the pool and retracted it with a yelp.

"This is colder than the glacier that froze off my toe, brother," he said. "Maybe Danielle has some kind of inner strength that we lack. I don't think I could swim through this pool."

"And besides," Danielle said, "to my knowledge, no man has ever successfully swum through these waters. I think you might have to worry about losing more than just a toe."

Panther snickered, and Cougar eyed the icy water nervously.

"I'll let you go, Danielle," Cougar said, "but I'm going in after you if you're not back in five minutes."

"Agreed," Danielle said. "Now, what do you think we should do with our food and water? If we carry a week's supply, our movement will be hampered."

"We'll take only what we need for one day and

leave the rest in the vehicle," Jaguar said. "We can come back for more if we need it. Or we can fast."

"Or, we can eat the food supplied by the machines," Danielle added.

Jaguar narrowed his eyes. "Or we can fast," he repeated.

They gathered what they needed from the vehicle, and Danielle gave Cougar a quick hug. She left the transmitter on top of her pile of old clothes. She entered the vehicle and said, "Close." She pressed her face against the window and crossed her eyes at Cougar. Then she said, "Back to the other side of the pool."

The vehicle entered the pool, battering ice shards out of the way.

"Temperature 1.0," Danielle said. She wanted to be as hot as possible before diving into the water. The temperature rose, and she immediately began to sweat. The air felt as hot as rising cinders from a fire, and she had to breathe through her mouth. Streams of sweat cascaded down her face by the time the vehicle emerged in the tunnel.

"Open," she said, "and temperature 0.5." She did not want the food and water in the vehicle to remain heated.

She leaped out of the vehicle, removed her sweat-soaked buckskin tunic, and dived into the water with her arms extended over her head. She clamped shut her eyes and mouth, and she screamed through closed lips. She kicked powerfully, even as her legs began to numb. The cold that tore at her skin was not the natural cold of iced-over ponds or falling snow. This was a synthetic cold, a manufactured cold, a cold that employed giant pistons to pump the warmth from her sinews. This cold pierced her flesh like icy syringes and seemed to wrench the red out of her blood.

She hauled herself through the submerged opening in the wall. She sprang off the bottom of the opening, but weakly, and poorly directed. She was not sure which way was up. Her lungs felt full of snow, and she did not know if she would be able to breathe again even if she made it to the surface. Her head ached as though nails were getting hammered into her skull. She did not remember such pain. Had she grown soft in the free nation? Had the pine-fragranced breezes and pure waters actually weakened her?

She panicked, realizing that she had been lost in her thoughts. She could no longer feel her arms and legs, and she did not know whether she was swimming or merely drifting to her death. She felt only the nails hammering deeper into her skull, their sharp points denting one another in the center.

A dull pressure around her wrists was her only indication that someone had seized her. She was hoisted to the surface and then out of the pool. She tried to inhale, but the air caught in her throat. She panted frantically, warming first her tongue, which began to prickle sharply. Then the prickles descended into her throat, allowing her to hoarsely gasp.

"Temperature 1.0," she croaked.

As the temperature soared, she was able to open her eyes and breathe deeply. She crawled into her old clothes, loosening the drawstrings to accommodate her enhanced musculature. She wiped her hand dry and put the transmitter in her pocket.

"It's a good thing we were all here," Jaguar said, shoveling sweat off his face with his hands. "After you stopped moving, Panther and I had to lower Cougar into the pool by his ankles."

Cougar lay on his side, shuddering convulsively and flexing his fingers. "Luckily, they only had to lower me to my waist," he moaned. "It's a good thing I have long arms."

"Temperature 0.5," Danielle said, hoping to disturb this block as little as possible. "I'm so disappointed in myself. I thought I was so much weaker a year ago, but I made it through the pool all by myself. This time, I would have died if you hadn't been here."

"I don't think so," Panther said, wringing sweat out of his braids. "You knew we were here to rescue you, so you didn't have to try as hard. If we hadn't been here, I think you would have made it."

Danielle strapped on her pouches and slung

her bow and quiver over her shoulder. She helped Cougar to his feet.

"Do you have a little more respect for my abilities now?" she asked.

"A lot more," Cougar said, folding his arms around her. Then he too slung his bow and quiver over his shoulder.

Cougar led them out of the room. They crept down the hallway, and the stench intensified. A side passage led to the left.

"Danielle, you came from the left," Cougar said, "but the warden came from straight ahead."

"Let's go straight," Danielle said. "I'm sure his method of entry was more pleasant than mine."

Cougar frowned. "There are tracks left by wheels, as of many carts, but there are no tracks of anyone pushing these carts."

"The carts are robotic," Danielle said. "They carry sewage. Let's hope we don't encounter any."

They continued down the hallway and eventually turned to the right. There, the hall ended in a closed door marked 3892. Danielle opened the door with the transmitter, and they cautiously left the building.

When the door closed behind them, Danielle said, "From this side, the door is unmarked and fairly well camouflaged. No wonder Roger couldn't see it. Now, we can call a taxi. Taxi!"

While waiting, her companions carefully observed the rough, concrete ground, the dingy walls of windowless buildings, and the glowing ceiling.

"People don't live here," Cougar. "What are all these structures for?"

"I don't know," Danielle said. "Maybe people lived here long ago. Maybe these buildings are factories or some other facilities run by machines. But even places that don't smell this bad have many inexplicable buildings. Whoever built the crypt nation must have had some reason for it."

A taxi appeared from an intersection. Cougar leapt in front of Danielle and aimed an arrow at it.

"It's okay," Danielle said. "It's unoccupied. And remember, the safety belts aren't venomous snakes. They're there to help us."

"I don't like them," Cougar said. "I'm going to cut mine off anyway."

Jaguar coughed and wheezed slightly as they entered the taxi. He took a swallow from his waterskin.

"When I return to the free nation, I will rejoice in every breath, such as I never did before," Jaguar said.

"The B4D block of precinct $x = -0.10$, $y = 0.37$, $z = -0.29$," Danielle said.

The taxi rolled into motion. Its occupants fingered the hilts of their knives and looked around nervously.

"There are no fresh tracks in sight, except for those of the sewage carts," Cougar said. "And yet

I feel more imperiled than when I wandered the brigand nation."

They came to a door to the tunnel network that interconnected every block in the crypt nation. The door opened, and when it closed behind them, they were immersed in blackness. Whether their eyes were opened or closed, the view was the same. The taxi accelerated to an alarming speed.

"Somehow, this seems scarier than it used to," Danielle said. She was wedged tightly between Cougar and Panther, but she still felt vulnerable to unseen attacks.

"Does anyone want to hear a ghost story?" Panther asked.

No one answered, and Panther rewove one of his braids.

8

Sometimes I think I could use some peace and quiet. And then I realize that peace and quiet are all I have, and what I could really use are some friends.

–Janet Peptide, The Harder I Try, the Harder I Fail

"We're slowing down," Cougar whispered. He thumbed his bowstring impatiently and listened to Jaguar's increasingly irritating wheezes. A murky, rippling light appeared ahead.

Jaguar said, "That looks like light shining through—"

"Water!" Danielle screamed, as a low wave crashed against the wheels of the taxi. "I need to shut the door before the tunnel floods, and we drown! Shoot flaming arrows at the door so I can read the identification number!"

The three brothers leaped from the taxi and splashed into knee-high, rising water. They strung pinches of tinder around their arrowheads as Danielle spun a narrow stick between her hands. She pressed the bottom of the spinning stick against a small board. Fragrant smoke began to rise from the wood dust that accumulated in a notch in the board. Finally, the heated dust congealed into a glowing ember. After stabilizing the small ember, Danielle passed it to Cougar, who ignited his tinder and shared the flames with Panther and Jaguar. By the time they loosed their arrows, the water had risen to their waists, and the taxi began drifting toward the tunnel wall.

The flame from one of the arrowheads sputtered, and the tinder from another arrowhead fell into the water before it came near the door. The light from the third arrowhead allowed Danielle to read the identification number. She tapped on the transmitter, and the door lowered, plunging the tunnel back into darkness.

"I've never seen this before," Danielle said, clambering onto the top of the bobbing taxi. "The warden must have flooded the whole block to sabotage the technicians' project. I didn't know he could do that. At least we know we're on the right track. Anything the warden hates so much must be good for us."

"Why don't we just drain out all the water so that we can go in?" Panther asked.

"If we release too much water into the tunnels, it could attract attention," Cougar said.

"And a pipe in the block might dump in new water faster than we can drain it out," Danielle said.

"So what do we do?" Jaguar asked.

"The technicians are very crafty," Danielle said. "I think they may have had time to leave some kind of clues before they escaped or drowned. This seems to be the way that heretical societies operate. I had to string together a lot of clues to find the path of ascension."

"Quiet!" Panther hissed.

They froze and listened to soft gurgles in the blackness.

"False alarm," Panther said. "I thought I heard a splash, but I think it was just water draining into the lower tunnels."

"And I don't hear the motor of any vehicle, nor smell the fumes," Cougar said. "Nor do I smell malnourished flesh, such as Danielle had when she first emerged. I think we'll be hard to sneak up on, even in the dark."

"Still, there's no reason to dally," Jaguar said. "Danielle, open the door just high enough for us to squirm through. Shut it behind us. Give us five minutes. Then open the door to let us out. We'll let you know what we found."

"Are you sure you can hold your breath so long?" Danielle said.

"Easily," Cougar said. "We study the breathing patterns of seals. We'll teach you one day."

"Alright," Danielle sighed. "Leave your bows and arrows with me. You won't be able to use them underwater. And you have your knives."

Danielle climbed down from the taxi and splashed through the darkness to gather the bows and arrows. The water had now receded to ankle height.

"Let me know when you're at the door," Danielle said.

"We're here," Panther said.

Danielle tapped the necessary buttons on the transmitter, and the door began to rise. Murky light glimmered through the water beneath the door. She heard Jaguar's raspy inhalation, and then the shadowy figures of the three brothers disappeared beneath the door. She typed the instruction to lower the door, and she stood alone in darkness.

She counted silently and listened anxiously to water trickling through the tunnel. She strained her ears. If she were killed now, the others would drown. She tried to hold her breath the whole time, to see how difficult it was, but she gave up after two minutes. She slid her fingers nervously along Cougar's bow.

Finally, the time came to open the door. The

brothers slithered through, and the door shut behind them. Jaguar rinsed his mouth with water from his waterskin.

"Crypt water tastes like something squeezed from a drowned man's lungs," Jaguar sputtered. "And not just because drowned men were actually floating in it."

"I think I found the clue," Cougar said. "I pried a talisman from a dead man's fingers. Danielle, take this. Tell us its meaning."

Danielle reached through the dark and received Cougar's offering. Then she laughed.

"This is no talisman!" she said. "This is a toothbrush!"

Cougar grunted. "At least he died with clean teeth," he said.

"Take what I found, Danielle," Jaguar said. "Based on your descriptions, I think it's a book. I found it shoved inside a ceiling pipe that was spewing the foul water."

Danielle took the book as Jaguar lit some tinder. Danielle squinted in the dim, smoky light. She brushed droplets from the drenched book.

"This is a ledger of volleyball scores," Danielle said. "There are hundreds of numbers. Secret information could be hidden in any number of ways. I just don't know if there are clues here, or how to decipher them if there are. I'd have to study it for hours or days before deciding whether there's any kind of pattern."

"Maybe someone shoved it into the pipe in a desperate attempt to stop the water," Cougar said. "The writing could be insignificant. I don't want to waste too much time on this."

"Then what do you suggest?" Jaguar said.

"Doesn't anyone want to know what I found?" Panther said.

"Of course," Danielle said. "What was it?"

"Well, I thought about what I'd do if I were a crafty person trying to leave a clue in a flooding block," Panther began. "I'd know that it would be difficult to swim far through the water, so I'd want to put the clue as close to the door as possible. After swimming in, I searched all around the door, always within several paces of it. I found nothing of consequence. I waited, disheartened, until the door opened. But as I crawled out, I slid my fingers along the bottom edge of the door. Something was carved on the underside of the door! What's more, I recognized some of the carvings as numbers on your transmitter. There were also symbols unknown to me, but I memorized them all. I can draw the whole message on Danielle's palm with my finger."

"Wait!" Cougar said. "It could be a trap. False information. The people who drowned obviously weren't able to open the doors. The doors must have been locked at some point. Maybe they still can't be opened from the inside. No one could have carved a clue on the underside of the door after the doors were locked. And before the doors were locked, how could anyone have known it would be necessary to leave a clue?"

"But what if the water started flooding, as a warning, before the doors were locked?" Jaguar said. "Whoever carved the clue may have known the block was going to flood while the doors were still working."

"Let's just see what the clue is, before Panther forgets it," Danielle said. "Panther, here's my hand."

As Panther moved his finger over Danielle's palm, she vocalized what he wrote.

"E7F -0.23 -0.29 -0.15. G0G -0.13 0.19 -0.01. B6E -0.46 0.73 0.29. H3C 0.22 0.38 -0.22."

"So what does that mean?" Cougar said.

"These are the locations of four blocks," Danielle said. "The first one is the E7F block in precinct $x = -0.23$, $y = -0.29$, $z = -0.15$."

"Why are four blocks identified?" Jaguar said. "Do we have to go from one to the other in order?"

"I don't know," Danielle said. "Maybe. But what do we look for in each?"

"But think of this," Panther said. "Each block is identified by four pieces of information: first the name of the block, and then the three coordinates of the precinct. Maybe these four blocks contain the same four pieces of information, in the same order, about the one block to which we ultimately have to go."

"That makes sense," said Danielle. "We just

have to hope that the warden doesn't know about these clues."

"If we're in a race for the encrypted destination, we have no time to lose," Jaguar said. "How much time will we need in each of these four blocks to find the necessary information?"

"It's impossible to say," Danielle said. "When I hunted the clues for the path of ascension, I sometimes spent hours searching. The information is hidden in ways you'd never imagine. The number of pieces in a puzzle. The number of hairs on a man's head. Of course, most of what you'll find in a block is completely irrelevant to the search. You have to sift through useless details. The information is supposed to be unobvious. It could take days just to find one coordinate."

"That's too much time!" Jaguar barked. "I say we split up. We each go to one of the four blocks and then reconvene with the information."

"That could be dangerous," Cougar said. "I don't want to leave Danielle unprotected."

"Me!" Danielle said. "I'm the one who grew up here. I'm the one with the transmitter. I'm the one who knows about guns. It's the rest of you I'm worried about! And you don't even know how to read. How will you ever find the hidden information?"

"We have our methods," Panther said. "We know, from the condition of the drowned corpses, that the block flooded about six weeks ago. When we enter a block, we'll examine all the tracks. We'll know if any people entered about six weeks ago. If they're still in the block, we'll see the recent tracks, and we'll follow them. None of the crypt-born have these skills. They don't even know they're leaving tracks. This task should be easy for us."

"Well, okay," Danielle said. "Then Jaguar's right. We'll save time if we split up."

"Agreed," Cougar said. "But you're going to the safest of the four blocks, Danielle. Can you tell which of the blocks is the safest?"

"The precincts seem to get increasingly dangerous towards the outer boundaries of the crypt nation," Danielle said. "I've never heard this explicitly, but I think we grow up with this knowledge. The safest block in the list is the G0G block in precinct $x = -0.13$, $y = 0.19$, $z = -0.01$. This is where the x coordinate is hidden."

"That's where you're going," Cougar said. "Don't argue. And I'm going to the most dangerous. Which is it?"

Danielle concentrated. "The B6E block in precinct $x = -0.46$, $y = 0.73$, $z = 0.29$. That'll be fairly perilous, but I've seen worse. You're looking for the y coordinate."

"I'm taking the next most dangerous," Jaguar said.

"That's the H3C block in precinct $x = 0.22$, $y =$

0.38, z = -0.22," Danielle said. "And you're looking for the z coordinate."

"Then I'll be searching, in the E7F block of precinct x = -0.23, y = -0.29, z = -0.15, for the name of the ultimate block," Panther said.

"Then I guess it's settled," Danielle said. "We'll just call for four taxis and be on our way."

"Where will we reconvene?" Cougar said.

"Oh!" Danielle said. "Good point. Let me come up with a random block. How about the C2I block of precinct x = 0.09, y = -0.03, z = 0.04?"

"We'll see you there," Jaguar said. "And one more thing. Give us our bows and quivers. We may require their services."

"Okay," Danielle said reluctantly. "But remember, most of the crypt-born are frail and innocent. They know nothing of our search. They'll ignore us if we're not too conspicuous. Try to blend in. Above all, try to be nice."

"Oh, don't worry," Cougar said. "I won't be seen killing anyone."

But he strummed his bowstring in the darkness, and Danielle wondered at the exact meaning of his words. When the taxis arrived, she was not entirely sorry to set out on her own.

9

I paced back and forth in my podiatrist's office and
asked if he ever felt any pain in his feet.
"Yes, I do," he said. "In fact, there's a pain in my foot
right now. But it's a pain I gladly endure to help a
patient."
"What could you possibly be talking about?" I
asked. "Why does your foot hurt?"
"You keep stepping on it as you pace," he said. "But
I've never seen you walk with such confidence, so I
didn't want to stop you."

–Janet Peptide, I Laugh To Keep from Belching

The warden's head thrashed from side to side on his pillow, and he groaned through clenched teeth. Sweat trickled between the rigid tendons and veins of his forehead and neck. His eyelids opened and shut, strenuously squeezing out thick tears.

"It's getting worse again, Wardy," Kristen Xylem said sadly. She mopped the warden's damp scalp with a cloth. "Have you killed a lot of people recently? It always gets worse after you kill people."

"I always kill people," the warden gasped. "It accomplishes little. New enemies arise faster than I can kill them. The slayings bring me neither satisfaction nor distress."

"I think they do bring you distress, Wardy," Kristen said. "Remember what the physician told you? She said she did all she could for you, but further improvement required you to forgive yourself."

"A charlatan! An imposter!" the warden hissed. "I only wish I'd killed her sooner." His fists clenched and unclenched.

"Wardy, why do you make things so hard for yourself?" Kristen said. "You improved, at least temporarily, after she treated you. What medicine was she injecting you with? Can't you get any more of it?"

"There was no medicine in those needles!" the warden said. "They were just solid pins! She kept pricking me and poking me, all the while babbling about stagnant energy and wiry pulses and other nonsense!"

"Well, I think she was helping you," Kristen said. "I think you should get another physician."

"I should kill them all to save the people from charlatanism!" the warden said. "Bedeviled by the charlatans, sick people have even forgone treatment from the medic vehicles, which our beloved ancestors, at the pinnacle of their glory, designed for our good health!"

"You don't seem very healthy to me," Kristen said, "and you summon medic vehicles all the time."

"Don't make sport of my suffering!" the warden shouted.

Kristen caressed his hollow cheek.

"I'm not making sport," she said. "I know better than anyone how you suffer. I'm just worried about you. Your condition has worsened over the past year."

The warden clawed the bed sheets.

"One year ago, I nearly achieved my most cherished goal," he said. "Then that misguided menace, Danielle Gasket, ruined everything! She selfishly destroyed the one vehicle intended to convey ordinary people along the path of ascension. Then she employed her dark arts to swim through frigid waters that freeze anyone else solid."

"I'm sure she's frozen solid too, just like the others you cast into the waters," Kristen said.

"No!" the warden snarled. "I commanded men to dip long, metal poles into those waters in order to search for Danielle's remains."

He gnashed his teeth and spat weakly. The spittle clung to his lips, and Kristen wiped it off.

"So?" she said. "What did they find?"

"The metal poles got so cold that they shattered, and so did the hands of the men," the warden said. "Then the men died. But before they did, they screamed something that sounded like, 'I feel nothing.'"

Kristen shrugged. "Maybe their hands had just gone numb."

"Danielle Gasket lives! I feel it!" the warden said. "From high above, basking in otherworldly pleasures, she mocks me! She revels in my pain! Through some infernal machinations, she poisons me and causes my suffering!"

"Wardy, stop ranting and raving!" Kristen said. "It scares me. Danielle can't affect you in any way, even if she did travel the path of ascension. And from what you've told me, your condition began long before she was even born. You're not making any more sense than the time you were crazy paranoid about conspiracies, and you accused even me of plotting against you. Do you remember what I did then?"

"You punched me in the mouth to stop me from ranting and raving," the warden said with a ghastly smile. "I kind of liked it."

"That's because something's terribly wrong with you," Kristen said. "You shouldn't like that. Now, try to get some rest. Try to breathe deeply, like the physician taught you. Breathe into the pain. Your muscles are all frozen around the affected area. At first, it will hurt to breathe it back to life, but then it will get better."

The warden gulped and shuddered, and his

eyelids fluttered closed. He breathed shakily and gasped as Kristen stroked his clammy face. Finally, after many minutes, his breath softened, his face relaxed, and even his hollow cheeks took on a little fullness.

A sudden pounding on the door jolted him awake. His mouth and eyes opened wide, and he looked about in confusion. Kristen sighed.

"Wardy! We have an urgent message!" called a man through the door

"Tell him to go away," Kristen whispered. "You need to rest. No one can tell you what to do."

"What? Who?" the warden said. He struggled to sit up as Kristen tried to soothe him.

"Someone comes with a credible report of Danielle Gasket," the man at the door said. "He asks to speak with you right away. He says that we have little time."

10

It hurts when you hang onto the edge of a cliff, not when you let go.

– Janet Peptide, Epistle from the Asylum

Panther chewed pine needles from his pouch as he rode a taxi through the tunnels. He breathed with his fingers close to his nose, trying to use the pine scent to mask the smell of poisonous exhaust. He silently repeated the name of the block containing the clue he sought: the E7F block in precinct $x = -0.23$, $y = -0.29$, $z = -0.15$. He needed to retain this information because, right now, he was going somewhere else.

He blinked and winced as the taxi entered a brightly lit block. He saw children playing cards, a woman walking on stilts, and a seated man weaving elaborate patterns into his extremely long hair. Panther secured his bow and quiver on his shoulders, and he stepped out of the taxi.

As the taxi departed, Panther strode quickly toward a blank wall and defensively turned his back toward it. A few unoccupied taxis meandered around pedestrians, and a speeding medic vehicle knocked over a house of cards before disappearing beyond the bend. Then an occupied taxi approached and slowed. Panther relaxed his grip on his bow and smiled.

A young man with narrow sideburns stepped out of the taxi and stared at Panther. The man's jaw hung open, and he tilted his head from side to side, as though daring Panther to disappear when viewed from different angles.

"You're here," the man said. "You're really here. Panther of the free nation."

"Brian Amygdala of the crypt nation," Panther said.

The two men embraced, then partially separated, holding each other by the upper arms.

"You look exactly how you did in my mind," Brian said. "I didn't think anyone could possibly be so muscular, and yet so sleek. So graceful, yet so powerful. How hollow and cadaverous I must appear to you."

"Actually, you're the healthiest-looking crypt-born I've seen so far," Panther said. "Have you been practicing the exercises I taught you?"

"Yes," Brian said, squeezing Panther's arms. "The breathing exercises. The calisthenics. The stretches. The meditations to ward off evil and purify the aura. Believe it or not, similar exercises are described in some obscure texts that I've found. I searched dozens of libraries and archives. I've accumulated a large collection. Would you like to see it?"

"Sadly, I have but little time," Panther said.

"I know," Brian said. "I've been reading your thoughts more easily than ever, now that you're here in the crypt nation. And that's how I know that you haven't been able to read mine. The pervasive buzz of machinery seems to be clouding your mind. As soon as you were assigned the E7F block in precinct $x = -0.23$, $y = -0.29$, $z = -0.15$, I rushed there by taxi. It is not so far. And I think I've discovered your clue."

"Really?" Panther said. "What is it?"

"The lighting in that block was a bit strange. It seemed a little too yellow. I issued verbal commands to change the lighting to the standard hue, red 0.1, yellow 0.6, blue 0.9. But nothing happened. I talked to some people on the block, and they said that the ceiling panels broke about six weeks ago. The panels won't change color, even when ordered to. Then I rushed back here and briefly changed the lighting to red 0.1, yellow 0.7, blue 0.9. The color perfectly matched what I'd seen in the other block."

"So the clue for me is 0.1, 0.7, 0.9," Panther said. "And this is supposed to encode the name of a block, which consists of a letter surrounded by two numbers. What is the seventh letter of your alphabet?"

"G," Brian said.

"So do you agree that the encrypted block name is 1G9?"

"Exactly," Brian said.

Panther smiled.

"Then I think you've bought us some time," Panther said. "I'm sure my companions can't have discovered their clues already."

"Then you'll come see my collection of texts?" Brian said.

Panther nodded, and he proceeded down the street with Brian, hand in hand.

"Why do you stare at the ground?" Brian asked.

"I thought you could read my mind," Panther said.

"I can, but only about half the time. I'm not sure why," Brian said. "Maybe I'll get better with practice."

"I stare at the ground to read tracks," Panther said. "You know, the tracks leave a record of everything the person was thinking and feeling. It's a complicated language, but I've begun to learn how to read it. I don't see any traces of hostile intent in these tracks. I think this is a safe block."

"That's good," Brian said. "Though I wouldn't mind a little adventure."

Panther sighed. "Adventure always sounds great, except for when you're in its midst. My adventure in the crypt nation has been placid so far, but that won't last forever."

"Take me with you?" Brian said, give Panther's hand a plaintive squeeze.

Panther shook his head, gazing a moment at people playing billiards in the middle of the road.

"I have trained as a warrior since childhood," Panther said. "I am prepared to fight as necessary. Even now, I may be attracting the attention of powerful enemies. I may be endangering you, even now."

"I don't mind the danger," Brian said.

"But I object to the danger you would face," Panther said. "I don't want to be responsible for your death. It will be better to communicate with you telepathically for the rest of my life, than to take you with me into danger for a few extra ill-fated hours together."

"But what of the other crypt-born, Danielle Gasket?" Brian said. "Why do accept her among your companions?"

"She is an exceptional case," Panther said. "She nearly perished many times as she sought to ascend. You would be unwise to follow her example. And now, she's been trained in the skills of the free nation for an entire year."

Brian sighed and tugged Panther's hand.

"Here, this is my building," Brian said.

They walked up three flights of crooked stairs. They entered a hallway, and Brian used a key to open the fourth door on the right. They walked into a room filled with chimes. The largest chimes hung from the ceiling all the way to the floor, while smaller chimes formed multilevel mobiles. As Brian and Panther shouldered their way through the chimes, the hollow, metallic tones cascaded all around them.

"I like chimes," Brian said.

"I knew that," Panther said, "by dint of my piercing insight."

Brian laughed.

"Just a little further," Brian said. "I keep the collection of texts in my bedroom because the chimes take up all the space in here."

They passed through a dense curtain of chimes, and they entered a room with a bed and a crowded bookcase. The chimes continued swaying and clinking behind them. Brian leaned closer to Panther.

"Are you really here just to read through my texts?" Brian asked.

"Of course not," Panther said. "I don't even know how to read."

Later, after the chimes had gone silent, Brian said, "What cruel force has kept us apart for so long?"

"The same merciful force that binds us now together," Panther said.

Panther stood up and walked over to the bookcase.

"You've read all of these?" Panther asked.

"No, I've only begun," Brian said, propping his shoulders up on a pillow. "They're very hard to understand. Half of the books are attempts to explain the meaning of the other half."

Panther pulled a thick book out from under a cluster of scrolls. He took it over to Brian.

"What is this one?" Panther asked.

"Oh, one of my favorites," Brian said. "It's The Doggerel of Janet Peptide, the most famous troubadour of antiquity."

Panther flipped through the musty pages.

"Read me this passage," Panther said.

Brian took the book and cleared his throat.

"One night, when I couldn't fall asleep, I started thinking about murky moonlight, and dark clouds, and cold raindrops, which were falling onto my face through a hole in the roof. It's funny what you think about when you can't fall asleep."

"This must have been written before the interment," Panther said.

"Yes," Brian said. "I can't understand many of the terms."

"Here," Panther said, pulling a handful of pine needles out of a pouch. "Perhaps this flavor will convey some of the spirit of the free nation."

"No," Brian said. "I'll never be able to eat from the food dispensers again if I taste the body of heaven."

"Perhaps you're right," Panther said, languidly dropping a few pine needles into his mouth. He chewed with soft, deliberate crunches.

"Take me with you," Brian pleaded again.

Panther shook his head.

"It's too dangerous," Panther said.

"Then stay with me," Brian said.

"I can't stay long," Panther said. "I'll die."

"I'll miss you when I reach for you, and you're not here," Brian said.

"If only I could cling to you as to an unbending pillar in a churning sea of tempests and changes," Panther said. "But the strength of my arm is required elsewhere."

"I'm afraid that if I blink, you'll disappear," Brian said.

"Then close your eyes and relax," Panther said. "I won't be able to leave without your knowledge. The chimes would give me away."

Brian closed his eyes and smiled.

"I always knew they'd be good for something."

Then he frowned.

Brian said, "A moment ago, when you said, 'I can't stay long, I'll die,' what exactly did you mean? Did you mean that you'll die if you stay too long? Or did you mean that you will die, and that's why you can't stay long?"

Brian waited for a response. His eyelids opened, and he saw that Panther was gone, though the chimes were motionless. Days later, he discovered a pouch of pine needles under his pillow.

11

Please, can anyone
Tell me where my needle is?
Pleaded the haystick.
–Janet Peptide's Greatest Doggerel

The newcomer to the block wore a cloak and leaned heavily on a staff. He frequently clutched his chest and bent close to the ground, and he wheezed with a harshness that he did not have to feign. With his eyes near the ground, he was better able to follow the tracks that had originated six weeks earlier.

"Sir, do you need any help?" a young woman asked the tracker. "There's a nice, quiet sculptor's studio across the street where you can rest until you catch your breath."

The tracker grunted and shook his head irritably. He ignored the woman and followed the tracks in and out of restaurants and gyms. He knew, from the tracks, that his quarry was a large man, swaggering and muscular, with a tendency to bump into people who failed to get out of his way. According to the tracks, this man occasionally sat on a bench by the road and conversed with someone in a vehicle. At one point, the vehicle's occupant swung a leg out onto the road and left a single footprint. The tracker gasped and teetered against his staff. He recognized the footprint. It belonged to the warden.

The tracker increased his pace when he came upon a more recent set of tracks. He limped from a decreasingly stooped position, and then he held his staff by his side and ran. He circumvented a circle of mean-faced men playing cards on the ground. He entered a building and ran up a flight of stairs. His quarry's tracks were abundant here. He followed the tracks to a door. He reached one hand to the stone knife beneath his cloak, and his other hand gave the door a quick shove. The door was locked.

The tracker squatted to better view the tracks. He identified a sequence of tracks leading further along the hallway. He came to a large room where a man played ping-pong by himself. He hit the ball, ran around the table, and hit the ball back to the other side. He wore a green vest, matching mittens, and matching hair.

"Hey," the man said to the tracker, "do you want to play ping-pong?"

"Sure," the tracker said. "Why not?"

The other man breathed heavily and wiped

sweat from his brow.

"I'm Russell," he said. "Who are you?"

"Jaguar."

"That's a weird name," Russell said.

"That's a weird comment," Jaguar said.

"So's that," Russell said, and Jaguar nodded.

Russell squinted as though trying to see inside Jaguar, and then he shrugged.

"Well, drop your staff and pick up the paddle, Jaguar," Russell said. "Zero serving zero."

Russell struck the ball forcefully. It bounced off Jaguar's side of the table. Jaguar smacked the ball with his paddle, and the ball whizzed directly into Russell's forehead.

"Ow!" Russell said. "Don't you know how to play? The ball has to hit the table."

"My apologies," Jaguar said.

Russell fetched the ball.

"One serving zero," he said.

Jaguar returned the serve by bouncing the ball hard off his own side of the table and right into Russell's forehead.

"Ow!" Russell said. "The ball has to hit my side of the table! Don't you know anything?"

"Again," Jaguar said, "my apologies."

"Two serving zero," Russell said.

Russell hit the ball with his paddle, but before the ball could hit the table, Jaguar hurled the table to the side, and the ball landed on the ground.

"My point!" Russell shouted. "You're not

allowed to throw the table to the side."

"Ah, how uncultured am I," Jaguar said. He returned the table to its original position.

"Three serving zero," Russell said.

Jaguar shoved the table into Russell, who dropped his paddle and fell on his back.

"That's not allowed either," Russell groaned, climbing to his feet and rubbing his ribs. "You can't move the table in any direction. Four serving zero."

Jaguar returned the ball so hard that it tore a hole through the net. Russell frowned.

"I've never seen that happen before," Russell said, "so I'm not sure who gets the point. I think I do, but I'd have to consult a rule book to be sure."

"I'll give you the benefit of the doubt," Jaguar said.

"I appreciate that," Russell said. "It's your serve."

"Zero serving five," Jaguar said, and he hit the ball onto the Russell's side of the table.

"Weren't you paying attention?" Russell said, catching the ball in his hand. "When you serve, you hit your own side of the table first."

"It's all becoming much clearer," Jaguar said. "Zero serving six."

Jaguar scored the next six points. He appeared totally absorbed in the game. He breathed heavily and stomped as he maneuvered around the table. After scoring his sixth point, he flung his paddle backwards without looking. The paddle struck the head of a man who had crept in and begun to draw a gun. The gunman collapsed.

"I was only pretending not to pay attention to my surroundings," Jaguar said to Russell. "I'm even better at self-defense than I am at ping-pong. And you know what I'm even better at than self-defense? Interrogation. So why don't you make this easy on yourself, and tell me what you know?"

Russell sneered and reached for the gun in his pocket. Jaguar again thrust the ping-pong table into Russell, who sailed through the air and thumped against a wall. He slid down the wall and bled from his nose, mouth, and ears.

"Too hard," Jaguar sighed, and he turned to the unconscious gunman behind him. Jaguar frowned. Something was unusual about the gunman's hands. Jaguar stared and then noticed that the gunman had six circles tattooed on each palm. Jaguar ran over to Russell and removed his green mittens. Russell, too, had six circles tattooed on each palm. Then Jaguar gasped. The final ping-pong score had been six-six. Did all this evidence point to an encrypted coordinate of 0.66? Or was it false information planted by the warden? Jaguar did not think the warden could have controlled the ping-pong score; if Jaguar had wanted to play seriously from the beginning, Russell would never have scored. But then, what mysterious power was in control?

Jaguar shook his head and dissolved into the shadows. Perhaps the pervasive, mysterious power made itself most obvious in the crypt nation, which needed it the most.

12

When I was growing up, I hated Sammy, the kid who lived next door. I'd always invite him over when I knew no one would be home, but Sammy never caught on, and he spent many happy hours ringing the doorbell.

– Janet Peptide, I Laugh To Keep from Belching

Danielle Gasket strode confidently, even arrogantly, along the streets of the crypt nation. She beheld the sunken eyes and stooped shoulders of the crypt-born. They shuffled about with a halting gait as though uncertain they could muster the energy to take one more step. They coughed, and they wheezed, and they rubbed their sore stomachs. Danielle wanted to feel pity, but instead she felt revulsion. How had she lived this way for so long?

She felt her bow and quiver bouncing on her shoulder. Her stone knife rested comfortingly against her thigh. And yet, how secure should she really feel? If she relaxed her vigilance for just a moment, a bullet could tear through her ribs.

Her fingers drummed the buttons on the transmitter in her pocket. As she walked, she kept two taxis and a leisure carriage in a defensive formation around herself. It was probably an unnecessary precaution, but she needed to practice her skills with the transmitter. She maneuvered through a group of old men who turned cartwheels while finger-painting directly on the street.

"Ice, ice, why, why twice?" one of the old men bleated to her.

"I already know that one," Danielle said irritably, but she was unnerved. Why had this old man repeated one of the clues that had helped her ascend? Did he merely say this to every stranger, playing his role in the elaborate apparatus that preserved the heretical information? Or had he recognized her as the high heretic?

Danielle frowned and turned down a side street where pedestrian traffic was lighter. She glanced over her shoulder to confirm that no one was following. Then she looked ahead and found a young man gawking at her.

"Is that really you?" he said, blinking in wonder. "Danielle?"

Danielle clamped her hand over his mouth and tackled him into a taxi.

"Never say that name where anyone can hear you," Danielle whispered. "I have enemies. It's a long story. In the tunnel, we can talk more safely. Don't say a word until I tell you it's okay."

Danielle kept her head low as she steered the taxi with the transmitter. She navigated around several large sculptures, a crowded trampoline, and a wrecked medic vehicle. Then she entered the tunnel. The taxi traveled rapidly for several minutes before she halted it. She waited in silence. She heard the rumble of an approaching vehicle, and she readied an arrow against her bowstring. Then the sound receded, and she relaxed.

"Okay," she said. "I think we're safe. For now. Though somehow, you've become linked to my perilous search. You'd better never return to that block. What were you doing there, anyway?"

"Listen, Danielle," the young man said. "I only recently moved to the block, and only at Tommy Farad's insistence. Remember him? He told me the strangest things. He said that you were safe, and out of reach of harm, but that Mom and Dad and I were now in danger. He said he could keep us safe, but I had to do exactly what he said. I thought he'd gone crazy, but he showed me his scars. That convinced me that there really is some kind of evil overlord. I don't understand why Tommy got tortured and then released, but I didn't want to think about it too much."

"But Derek, how did you get Dad to agree to move?" Danielle said. "You know how protective he is of his vase collection."

"I moved the whole thing one night while he was sleeping," Derek said. "It took all night. He must have hundreds of vases now. I had to sneak in and out of his room, which he keeps full of orange vapor at all times. His asthma has gotten quite bad. I tried to hold my breath while I was in there, but my throat was raw and my eyes were red by the time I finished."

"And Mom? What did you tell her?" Danielle said.

Derek shrugged. "She was tired of that old place even before I was born. She was excited to move. She wanted to help move the vases, but her hands have gotten really shaky, and I wouldn't let her."

Danielle sighed. "What did you tell them about me?"

"They were really worried when you stopped visiting," Derek said. "So I started forging letters from you. You know, my handwriting still looks exactly like yours. According to your letters, you found a new hobby, needlepoint, and you love it so much, you don't have time to do anything else. So I visit you to pick up the letters, but otherwise, you and your needlepoint friends are a very insular society."

"Needlepoint!" Danielle said. "That's the best you could come up with? Do you really think that suits my personality?"

"Dull, uninspiring, and mildly dangerous," Derek said. "I'd say that suits you perfectly."

Danielle laughed. "Well, thank you for filling in during my absence. Unfortunately, I can't stay long. I need to return to your block to look for something. I'll call a second taxi so we can return separately. If you see me again, just pretend you don't know me. If Tommy said it's safe for you to live there, I'll believe him, but don't take any unnecessary risks."

"Wait," Derek said. "I think I have what you're looking for. Tommy gave me this, and he told me to give it to you if I saw you."

Derek handed Danielle a transmitter.

"A transmitter!" Danielle said. "Do you know how to use this?"

"No," Derek said. "Tommy told me not to push the buttons.

"So Tommy's really deeply involved in this whole thing," Danielle said. "I wonder what secret this transmitter holds? I think I should explore this on my own. I don't want to needlessly endanger you."

"And I don't want to be needlessly endangered," Derek said. "But it's been good seeing you. If you run into Tommy, I hope you can help keep him safe. You now look like some kind of warrior from the troubadour ballads."

"I am," Danielle said.

She stepped out of the taxi.

"Keep practicing your needlepoint," Derek said.

"Keep practicing your sarcasm," Danielle said.

The taxi drove away, leaving Danielle alone in darkness and corrosive exhaust.

"Leisure carriage," she said.

After several moments, she heard an approaching rumble. The she saw the blue glow of the interior panel of the leisure carriage. It stopped next to her. She read its identification number, 7272, and then she typed instructions on the transmitter Derek had just given her. Nothing happened. She aimed the transmitter carefully and retyped the instructions, but the leisure carriage remained still. Danielle shifted her weight in frustration. How could a broken transmitter conceal secret information? Should she bust it open to see if anything was hidden inside?

Then she had another idea. Maybe this transmitter could be used only for a single instruction. That seemed like a possible way to communicate secret information. Danielle began typing all the vehicular instructions she knew: commands to accelerate, decelerate, and move forwards or backwards. Next, she typed commands to make the vehicle turn 90 degrees to the left or right. Next, she proceeded to type commands to make the vehicle turn through other angles. When she typed 7272, the command to make the vehicle turn 45 degrees to the left, the leisure carriage spun obediently.

Danielle rubbed her head. 7272 was also the identification number of this leisure carriage! Had some technician, secretly allied with Danielle, caused this particular carriage to arrive? Danielle seemed to have confirmation that the hidden coordinate was 0.72. Now that she had extracted the message from the faulty transmitter, she placed it in front of a wheel of the leisure carriage. She used her regular transmitter to control the carriage, which crunched over the faulty transmitter and rumbled onward through the darkness.

13

*I try not to be competitive. In fact, I try harder
than anyone else.*

– Janet Peptide, The Harder I Try, the Harder I Fail

Danielle sat on a bench in the designated block.
She fidgeted and looked around at the pedestrians,
the vehicles, and the other people seated on
benches. Where were Cougar, Panther, and
Jaguar? What was taking them so long? Danielle
fingered the hilt of her knife and wondered what
she would do if they never arrived.

"Try to pay more attention to what's around
you," Cougar whispered in her ear.

"Yike!" Danielle said. "How did you sneak up
like that? I was trying to pay attention."

Then her jaw dropped, as she saw that Cougar held an armful of trophies.

"What did I say about not being conspicuous?" Danielle said.

Cougar shrugged.

"I didn't want to disappoint my fans," Cougar said.

Danielle groaned and wrapped an arm around Cougar's neck.

"Sit down," she said. "Let me see what you won these for. Wrestling. Boxing. Weight lifting. Bellowing. Bellowing? That's a competitive sport? Jumping rope. Seriously? That's a game for little girls."

"They cry when they lose," Cougar said.

Danielle sighed. "Did you find what you were looking for?" she said. "And I'm not talking about the admiration of spectators or the tears of defeated children."

"Yes," Cougar said. "I got it."

"How did you find it?" Danielle whispered. "You didn't kill anyone, did you?"

"I did what was necessary," Cougar said. "And sometimes what's necessary isn't very nice."

Danielle looked away.

"You know what it's like," Cougar said. "You left your own trail of corpses when you ascended."

"I know, I know," Danielle sighed. "I just don't like thinking about it."

"Here they come," Cougar said.

"Who? Panther and Jaguar?" Danielle said, looking in all directions. "I don't see them."

"I have the feeling I get when my own tracks are being followed," Cougar said.

Danielle concentrated on her surroundings. A leisure carriage passed to the right. Three children chased after it, trying to hit it with balls. A robotic wagon full of ladders passed to the left. Ladders occasionally fell out of the wagon and clattered on the ground. A medic vehicle passed in front of the ladders, and after it had passed, two of the ladders were gone. Danielle gasped and looked under her bench. Panther and Jaguar were hiding there.

"You'll teach me how to do that, won't you?" Danielle said. "I'm not nearly so good at blending in."

"But you are!" Panther said, crawling smoothly to his feet. "Before you spoke, I didn't even see you up there!"

Danielle laughed and wrapped her arms around Panther and Jaguar.

"Trophies, brother?" Jaguar said to Cougar. "Was that really necessary?"

"You're incorrigible," Panther told Cougar.

"I think the reproach would be a lot more effective if its target were intelligent enough to understand it," Jaguar said.

Cougar feigned a stupefied expression.

"Did you find what you needed?" Jaguar said.

Cougar and Danielle nodded.

"Then let's go," Jaguar said.

"Can I keep my trophies?" Cougar asked.

Jaguar threw them against a wall, and a maintenance drone arrived to slurp the broken pieces through its green hose.

"Why are you so mean?" Cougar said, but Jaguar ignored him and called a taxi.

The four of them got in the taxi and, after hushed discussion, directed the taxi toward the 1G9 block of precinct x = 0.72, y = -0.38, z = 0.66.

"The block I searched had been infiltrated by the warden," Jaguar whispered in the darkness of the tunnels. "I can't be sure that the warden doesn't know the z coordinate. Did the rest of you notice any signs of the warden?"

"I didn't," Danielle said, "and the x coordinate was delivered to me in a way that would be difficult to corrupt. I think it's impossible that the warden is on our trail."

"So we hope," Cougar said ominously.

They rode in silence and emerged into a noisy, smoky block. A large, central building belched black clouds from several pipes. The pipes rattled as loud pops rang from the building. Several pedestrians walked slowly, breathing through rags and coughing. Jaguar coughed, spat, and stepped out of the taxi with a fierce, stoic expression.

"See the tracks! So easy to follow on this sooty

floor," Cougar said, climbing out of the taxi. "There! Two people arrived together about six weeks ago. One, a young boy, only eight or ten. The other, an old woman in her mid-seventies."

"No, her late fifties," Panther said, squatting near the ground. "Remember how the poor nutrition and venomous air accelerate aging."

Cougar squinted and nodded.

"I'm glad you're with me," Danielle said. "There must be dozens or hundreds of people living in this block, walking all over the place. I can't isolate the two sets of tracks that you see."

"You'll learn," Cougar said. "Just follow us for now."

They walked briskly past several libraries, artists' studios, and a restaurant. They slowed to avoid getting caught in the middle of a group of people playing catch with several tubas. The tubas were severely dented. Danielle and her companions continued past two apartment buildings.

"The boy lives in that building," Cougar said. "He's in there now. The woman visited him within the last hour, but she continued that way."

"We follow her," Jaguar said.

They turned left and continued down a street where the smoke was very thick. Jaguar choked and grabbed his bow as though for strength. Next, they turned right and saw several benches facing a warehouse.

"That's her," Cougar said, "on the middle bench."

A woman with short, silver hair was playing cat's cradle with a string. She turned and looked quizzically at the trackers. Nearby, a maintenance drone struggled to pull its hose out from under a pile of metal beams.

"She's here to help us," Panther said. "I thought I saw it in her tracks, but it's clear on her face."

"We'll see about that," Cougar grumbled. "We need more proof than cherub-nation flimflam."

"Let me handle this," Danielle said. "We don't want to frighten her."

"I'm right here," the woman said. "I can hear you talking about me."

"I'm sorry," Danielle said. "That's terribly rude of us."

"I don't care about etiquette," the woman snapped. "I just need to confirm that you're not in league with the warden."

"That's what we need to confirm about you," Cougar said.

They glared at each other as the factory clanged in the background.

"You are not to be trusted," the woman said forcefully.

Cougar drew his knife, and Danielle grabbed his wrist.

"Enough!" Panther said. "She is here to help us, but that is her secondary purpose. Her primary purpose is to protect the boy. I can read it on her face."

The woman raised an eyebrow and nodded approvingly.

"You can read faces even better than I can," she said. "Maybe I was wrong about your brother."

Cougar grimaced but sheathed his knife.

"Follow me," the woman said. "We'll go somewhere we can speak more freely. You are the ones we've been waiting for."

They followed the woman back through the smoke-filled street and into the apartment where the boy lived. They climbed two flights of stairs and into a hallway. Two men in soiled clothing lay on the floor, staring vacantly at the ceiling.

"Yellow pills," the silver-haired woman said disdainfully, stepping over the men.

"I'll explain later," Danielle whispered to the three brothers. They kept their hands on their knives as they stepped over the men.

The woman approached the third door on the right. She knocked in an elaborate pattern. Then came the sounds of at least half a dozen bolts sliding open. A young boy opened the door and smiled.

"Angela!" he said.

"Hello again, Leon," Angela said. "They've finally come."

Danielle, Jaguar, Cougar, and Panther introduced themselves and entered the apartment. Leon bolted the door behind them, and they sat on metal chests. The floor was littered with gears, hammers, screwdrivers, wires, and metal rods. It was impossible not to step on things while walking across the room.

"I had a hunch you'd be coming today," Leon said. "I spent all morning cleaning."

"It really shows," Cougar said.

Danielle glared at him, but Leon apparently missed the sarcasm.

"I'm the technicians' guildmaster," Leon said. "The former guildmaster drowned in the flooded block. Before she drowned, she was able to smuggle out the design of the ultimate machine. I succeeded in following the design."

He stood and reached into the chest he'd been sitting on. He pulled out a small music box and wound it up. Horrendous screeching sounds filled the room.

"The music is my improvement upon the original design," Leon said. "These sweet melodies don't have any effect on the machine's real purpose. The real purpose, as you know, is to produce the elixir that you need. In fact, some in my guild believe that the real purpose of the entire crypt nation is to produce this machine. You see, it took hundreds of generations of experimentation to arrive at this design. Where else but in a miserable dungeon would talented people focus all their efforts, their whole lives, on such a tedious and thankless task? If my forebears had been free to breathe fragrant air, and to taste sweet, refreshing flavors, they may have forsaken their burden, and this machine would never have been built."

"This is all very fascinating, and I hope some day the historical controversy gets resolved," Jaguar said, "but we're in a bit of a rush. Could you please just give us the elixir and send us on our way?"

"If only it were that simple," Leon said. "You see, one crucial part is missing from this machine. We're missing a crystal, the only one of its kind, and it's deep in the flooded block. The last guildmaster drowned trying to retrieve it."

"We can hold our breath for a really long time," Cougar said. "I'm sure we'll be able to swim underwater and retrieve the crystal."

"Really?" Leon said. "After you enter the block, you have to pass five streets, turn left, take the next right, and enter the fourth building on the left. Then you go up five flights of stairs, go in the third door on the right, shove the grand piano off a carpet, open the trap door under the carpet, and remove a key from the box you find there. Once you take that key, a mechanism is set into motion that will cause the entire block to explode seven minutes later."

"Won't the explosion alert the warden?" Danielle said.

"No," Leon said. "It's a gentle explosion. Soft. Soothing, as long as you're not in it. Once you have the key, leave the building, turn left, pass four streets, turn right, enter the second building on the left, go up two flights of stairs, use the key to open the third door on the left, go to the chest of drawers filled with bricks, push it out of the way, go through the doorway, and then find the crystal in a pillow under an anvil."

"Okay, maybe I was wrong," Cougar said. "Maybe I can't hold my breath that long."

"Then must we drain the water out of the block?" Jaguar said.

"No," Angela said. "You must drain as little water as possible into the tunnels. The warden will know if a lot of water enters the tunnels."

"Besides," Leon said, "the pipes flooding the block can supply water faster than you can drain it out."

"Then what are we to do?" Panther said.

"We must use the amphibious vehicle that we left in the path of ascension," Danielle said. "It's the only way."

"I don't know," Jaguar said. "It's the vehicle that the warden's really after. What if this is all an elaborate ruse to lure out the vehicle?"

"We have no other choice," Danielle said. "If we don't use the vehicle, we must return empty-handed."

Jaguar rubbed his head.

"Very well," Jaguar said, "but I don't want to leave Leon's machine unguarded. Panther and I will stay here with Leon and Angela. We will set traps. Be careful when you return. I don't know what anvils and grand pianos are, but I infer that they are heavy and can be useful in bone-splintering deadfalls. Danielle, you and Cougar will retrieve the crystal."

"We can ride the vehicle into the flooded block," Danielle said, "but we'll have to open the hatch to swim out for the crystal. How can we control the vehicle when we're in the water? Won't the water ruin my transmitter?"

"No," Leon said. "Water does not harm the transmitter. However, the amphibious vehicle does not move when the hatch is open. It's a safety feature, see? So the hatch must close before the vehicle starts moving again, whether or not you're in it. Similarly, the hatch won't open while the vehicle is moving."

Danielle drank from her waterskin and looked at Cougar.

"Are you ready?" she said.

He grinned and nodded.

"I know something of the path of ascension," Angela said. "Did you leave your vehicle on the other side of the ice pool?"

Danielle nodded.

"That was wise," Angela said, "though you must again swim through that deathly water. I can heat your body so that you will more easily withstand the cold. I am the guildmaster of the physicians. We are even more secretive than the technicians, so you probably haven't heard of us. Our arts, however, can be even more useful than theirs."

"It's true that I've never heard of physicians," Danielle said, "but I'm willing to try anything to make that icy swim less torturous."

"Give me your hands," Angela said.

Danielle extended her hands, and Angela removed a packet of long pins from her pocket. She inserted pins in the webbing between Danielle's fingers. Then she inserted several pins in Danielle's ears. Cougar stared suspiciously.

"I've seen similar practices in the cherub nation," Panther said.

"That does nothing to increase my confidence," Cougar grumbled.

"Leave these in for five minutes," Angela said. "Remove them when you begin to feel hot. You must enter the ice water within half an hour, or you will die of overheating."

"Thanks for the warning," Danielle said, and she turned to Cougar. "I suppose we'd better go."

An especially loud thump rang from the factory outside, reminding them all of the smoky, suffocating air. Jaguar cleared his throat and spat into his palm.

14

If you ever need cash, just ask me, because money
seems to follow me wherever I go. So do the police,
as well as the rightful owners of that money.
– Janet Peptide, I Laugh To Keep from Belching

"I don't like this," Cougar said as they rode
through the darkness. "It feels like a retreat. I
never like returning to an earlier position before
my objective is reached."

"I don't like it either," Danielle said, plucking
pins out of her hands and ears. "But I don't see
any other choice."

Danielle panted and wiped sweat from her
brow.

"I can feel the heat radiating from you like a fire,"

Cougar said. "Angela's medicine is frighteningly powerful."

"I never thought I'd look forward to a plunge in the ice pool, but I'm starting to," Danielle said.

By the time they exited the tunnel, sweat from Danielle's bald head was splashing onto her shoulders. She drank thirstily from her waterskin and groaned. Seizing her transmitter, she guided the taxi through the reeking block. She raised the secret door to the hallway leading to the ice pool.

"This is very good," Cougar said, staring at the ground as they entered the hallway. "No one has been here since we left." Still, he held an arrow against his bowstring.

When they arrived at the ice pool, Danielle was sweating so fiercely that her nostrils flooded when she tried to inhale through her nose. Hot, salty sweat streamed over her lips as she gasped for breath. Her eyes stung, and droplets of sweat lingered on her eyelashes. Her earlobes were sweating. Her toes were sweating. She jumped out of the taxi and slid on the sweat coating her feet. She stumbled and nearly fell into Roger Clade's cadaver. She slung off her drenched clothes and dived into the ice pool.

A red coal dropped onto a frozen lake! A flaming torch plunged into the snow! For several seconds, Danielle was overwhelmed with relief, but she dared not relax. She kicked furiously while tearing through the water with her arms.

When she pulled herself through the submerged opening in the wall, the cold began seeping in. Her skin burned with cold. Her throat seemed to be in the grip of a tightening vise. She felt her panicked pulse in her neck, and her limbs suddenly felt too stiff to move. Had she squandered her advantage? Had she already frozen solid, with a mind helpless to do anything but feel pain and fear?

Then she felt the tips of the physician's pins as though they were still in her skin. She remembered, as though from distant antiquity, the feeling of warmth. She kicked, though her legs were numb below the knees. She pulled, though her arms were numb throughout. Her face felt lashed by torrential hailstones, and she was unsure whether she had surfaced. She heard an agonized scream and knew it had to be her own. She fought her way blindly to the edge of the pool. She flopped out of the water and shivered. As feeling returned to her skin, she became aware that she was abrading her elbows and heels against the concrete floor.

"Temperature 1.0," she said to the vehicle.

Sobbing and gasping, she crawled into the vehicle and quivered. Before recovering fully, she planned her next step. The vehicle contained a six-day supply of food and water. Perhaps it would be best to leave the supplies on this side of the ice pool where no one could steal them. She unloaded the supplies and settled into the vehicle.

"Temperature 0.5," she said, "and take me back to the other side of the pool."

The hatch closed. The vehicle lurched into the pool and descended, drifting downwards through jiggling bubbles and murky darkness. It passed through the opening, wheezed as it ascended, and splashed out of the pool.

"Open," Danielle said.

The hatch opened, and she walked over to her clothes and put them on. She confirmed that her transmitter was still in her pocket.

"Cougar, where are you?" she said.

"Just practicing stealth," he said from right behind her.

Danielle spun around.

"Wow!" she said. "You're so good at that. It's a good thing you're on my side."

"It's a good thing," he said, but he looked away as he said it, as though searching for enemies among the shadows. Still looking away, he handed Danielle her bow, quiver, and pouches.

"What are you looking for?" Danielle said.

"I don't know," he said. "I'm just worried that things may be different from how they seem. Just a false premonition, perhaps. Let us not dwell upon it."

They climbed into the amphibious vehicle and stated the coordinates of the flooded block. The hatch closed, and the vehicle accelerated down the hallway.

"I think we're really safe in this vehicle," Danielle said. "The window must be really strong the withstand the weight of water. Maybe it's even bullet-proof."

"Maybe," Cougar said, but he remained vigilant as they left the building and headed toward the tunnel.

They entered the darkness, though this vehicle had an illuminated panel that now seemed conspicuous. Danielle shielded her face from the light.

They rode a moment through the silence, and then Danielle asked, "What's your favorite thing about the crypt nation so far?"

"You," Cougar said.

An odd huskiness in his voice made Danielle's neck prickle, and she wished she had Panther's ability to read intentions.

15

Face what no one else has faced!
Stabilize the toxic waste!
Gather waste from rock and mud!
Ransom forests with our blood!
Swimming through the poisoned lakes,
Ruing all our past mistakes,
Until the sullied river clears,
We'll wash the landscape with our tears!
–Janet Peptide's Greatest Doggerel

A murky light expanded up ahead, and the vehicle began to struggle against the rising wave of water. Danielle tapped on the transmitter to maximize the vehicle's efforts. Fighting against the current, the vehicle entered the flooded block, and Danielle made the tunnel door lower behind them. She directed the vehicle along the streets according to Leon's instructions. Papers, plastic blocks, and bloated corpses floated through the water.

"I can swim faster than you," Cougar said, "and you know how to use the transmitter, so I suggest the following. When we get to the building containing the key, take a deep breath and open the hatch. That will be the last breath we take until we leave the block. I'll swim into the building to get the key. You close the hatch. The vehicle will be full of water, but it won't move if the hatch is open.

"I expect to able to retrieve the key in two minutes. We'll want to go as quickly as possible to the crystal because we'll be running out of breath. Arrange for the vehicle to be speeding by the building when I emerge with the key. I'll grab onto the outside of the vehicle and ride to the building with the crystal. Again, I think it will take me two minutes to return with the crystal, so speed past the building when I'm coming out. We'll be really low on breath at this point and will be in a hurry to leave the block."

Danielle sighed.

"Okay," she said, "though I'm scared. I don't like thinking about getting sealed in a vehicle full of water."

"Then don't think about it," Cougar said with a smirk.

The vehicle slowed and paused.

"This is the building with the key," Danielle said. "You remember Leon's instructions."

Cougar nodded and placed his bow, quiver, and pouches on the floor of the vehicle. He hesitated over his knife and decided to leave it on his belt. He slowly inflated his lungs. Danielle did the same and, to save breath, opened the hatch by use of the transmitter instead of a vocal command.

A heavy wall of water crashed against them and filled the vehicle. The impact slammed Danielle's head against the seat and ripped the transmitter from her hand. Panicked, wide-eyed, she groped for it, not seeing it, until Cougar handed it to her with a look of annoyance. Then he kicked off the seat and was gone.

Danielle typed the command to close the hatch. She fought the impulse to swim out at the last minute. Now she was sealed in, embedded in water like an insect in amber. She allowed a small puff of air to bubble out of her nostrils. She was already desperate for breath. This was very bad.

She tried to focus on her urgent task. She tapped buttons on the transmitter. The vehicle turned around, traveled about a hundred yards, and then turned around again. Danielle paused and exhaled a little more air. Then she typed the instruction to accelerate to the greatest speed.

The vehicle wobbled and then jetted forward. A floating rag thumped into the vehicle's window. The rag clung briefly and then streaked upward.

Cougar soared out of the building. He was as fast as a seal, as fast as a shark. He was a little ahead of schedule. He spun to face the vehicle, which hurtled toward him. He smiled and winked at Danielle. He drifted upward, riding the current pushed forward by the vehicle. He spread his arms like the talons of an eagle and then seized the vehicle as it passed just below him. Through the window, Danielle could see his legs, pointing forward like a battering ram.

They passed four streets and then began arcing to the right. Danielle released a little more air from her lungs. Her vision began to dim, and her chest burned like the air above a fire. She continued to use the controller to refine the motion, turning to the right and decelerating as they approached the building with the crystal.

Cougar kicked off the vehicle with a thud and disappeared into the building. Danielle released more air. Her lungs were nearly empty, and she struggled not to inhale. She was sure that she was crying, though her tears vanished into the flood. Her arms and legs began to numb, and her heartbeats tore her chest like knives. Still, she typed commands into the transmitter. The vehicle slowed, spun around, and passed the building that Cougar was in. The vehicle spun around again and began to accelerate.

Involuntarily, Danielle swallowed some of the fetid water. She gagged and shook, trying to blink the darkness from her eyes. She rapidly approached Cougar's building, but he had not yet emerged. Would she have to wheel around and come back for him?

At the last minute, Cougar surged from the building. He grabbed onto the vehicle's window with one hand. His fingers slid, squealing, to the edge of the window, but then found a secure grip. He fluttered behind the vehicle like a streamer.

The vehicle swiveled to the right. Now there was a clear shot to the tunnel door, though they first had to cross 11 streets. Unable to stop herself, Danielle swallowed some more water, gulping it, breathing it, filling her lungs as well as her stomach. She would be unconscious before entering the tunnel. She typed a sequence of commands that would be executed after a specified delay.

Then her eyes closed. Her body felt heavy. Sick. Her throat felt raw. She couldn't move. Why couldn't she move? She couldn't move her little finger; she couldn't open her eyes; she couldn't make herself breathe. She knew she wasn't breathing. She knew she needed to breathe.

She heard a shrill pounding, and she shuddered. She managed to open her eyes, though the effort sent sharp pains through her head. She was still inside the flooded vehicle, but the vehicle was in the tunnel, and Cougar was standing outside of the vehicle, slamming his knife into the window. Her commands had been successfully executed: the tunnel door had opened in time to let the vehicle through, then the door closed to keep the tunnel from flooding, and then the vehicle decelerated to allow Cougar to safely dismount. She had forgotten only one command. The command to open the hatch.

Cougar saw her eye open, and he screamed something, as he continued to pound the window with his knife. Danielle couldn't hear him through the window, and her ears were full of water. She gulped water, and gulped and gulped again, and her eyes began to close once more. Her heartbeats sounded liked rusted gears grinding to a halt, and there was severe pain, terrible pain, and Danielle wasn't even sure whose pain it was.

Then her eyes widened. Where was the transmitter? While she lived, she still had a chance to open the hatch and save her own life. She tried to turn her head but could not. She could only move her eyes, and with her eyes stretched all the way to the side, she saw her fingers frozen around the transmitter, already sealed in the stiffness of death. She tried to force her fingers to move, but they ignored her. The harder she tried, the more pain and frustration she felt. In resignation, she realized that she did not even remember the command to open the hatch. 2791? Or 4582?

She saw total darkness, though she did not remember closing her eyes. She did not hear anything. She did not feel anything, not even her own body. So maybe this was death.

She had not lived to return to the free nation, though she had succeeded in retrieving Cougar and the crystal from the flooded block. For others, further adventures awaited. For others, there would be further joys and further sorrows; further embraces, further pleasures, and further struggles. But for her, there would be only darkness, and total surrender.

And in surrender, she felt the bliss that surpasses understanding, the bliss she had felt only one time before, under the influence of a yellow pill. And now, just as then, the bliss collapsed into nausea. She retched, seemingly for minutes, and then gasped for breath...and the breath came. She gasped again, and again, and again, as Cougar supported her.

"You should've told me that the vehicle responds to vocal commands from the outside," Cougar said. "I could've gotten you out earlier. I would've told the hatch to open in the first place, instead of trying to batter through the window."

Danielle gulped air, and sensation returned to her fingers and toes. She felt the warmth of Cougar's bald head against her own.

"I'm alive," she said. "I'm breathing."

16

Once I dreamed that a polar bear was chasing me across the tundra. Right before it sank its fangs into my tender flank, a look of recognition and mild confusion flashed across its face. When I woke up, the snow was cool and invigorating beneath my white paws. I saw, in the distance, a small, self-loathing wretch shivering and wandering about aimlessly. My stomach growled, and I set out on the hunt.

– Janet Peptide, I Laugh To Keep from Belching

The amphibious vehicle entered a block filled with black smoke and the clanging of unseen machinery. The vehicle's hatch opened. Two bald heads were visible above the water filling most of the vehicle. They smiled.

"We're back!" Danielle said. "I nearly died, but don't mention it. Always ready to give my life in the call of duty."

Panther looked up from the transmitter that he was using to control a maintenance drone.

"Look what Leon taught me!" he said. "I'm getting really good."

The maintenance drone inhaled a small ball through its green hose, spat the ball straight up in the air, and caught it in its hose. Jaguar shook his head and looked away in annoyance. Cougar jumped, dripping, from the water, and he began chasing the drone in circles.

"And look what else I learned!" Panther said.

Still operating the transmitter with one hand, he took a crayon and a scrap of paper and wrote, "Hi Danielle!"

"Panther! That's wonderful!" Danielle said, emerging from the water with her bow.

"Don't encourage him," Jaguar grumbled.

"Leave him alone," Danielle said. "He's a fast learner. How about you? Have you been gainfully occupied while we were gone?"

"I have," Jaguar said. "I've been disparaging my little brother's worthless new hobbies."

"It's true," Panther said. "He's done it tirelessly."

A man with a long, gray beard approached, squinting at the vehicle.

"What kind of vehicle is this?" he demanded.

"I've never seen anything like it."

"No?" Danielle said. "Remember how our forebears, in their, um, illustrious glory, invented the, ah, bathtub taxi? So that when you're really busy, you can travel and bathe at the same time? In their stupefying wisdom and boundless love for us, they made only a few bathtub taxis so that, er, unattended children wouldn't accidentally drown."

The man squinted at Danielle. His lip twitched, and he pulled a long, pointy pair of scissors from his pocket. Cougar, knife poised for piercing, was instantly behind the man.

"I remember now," the man said. "It's been a long time since I heard anyone mention a bathtub taxi. I think I was a child. They warned me not to drown myself if I saw one."

He ambled away, trimming his beard as he walked. He disappeared beyond swirling wisps of black smoke.

"I don't think the factory makes anything besides smoke and noise," Panther said. "There are no doors, and no tracks leading into it, either of people or machines."

Jaguar spat thick, black spittle onto the ground. The maintenance drone extended its hose eagerly.

"Leave it!" Jaguar barked. "Let's make the elixir and get out of here."

"Here," Cougar said, handing Jaguar the crystal.

"I'll stay and guard the vehicle."

"I'll go alone," Jaguar said. "I placed so many traps around Leon's workshop, it's a little dangerous for anyone else. An anvil is liable to swing out of the closet and smear someone along the opposite wall."

Coughing hoarsely, Jaguar departed.

"I hope the elixir's ready soon," Danielle said. "The crypt nation seems to be wearing on him."

"Angela offered to help him," Panther sighed, "but he refused treatment."

As they waited, several women set up bowling pins nearby and began to bowl. A couple of the women came to gawk at the amphibious vehicle.

"One of the rare bathtub taxis," Danielle said. "One of the many great triumphs of our forebears."

The women nodded wisely and returned to their game.

"While you were away," Panther said, "I decided to taste some of the so-called food from the dispensers. I spat it out, of course. I just wanted to know what it was like for the crypt-born."

"Ugh!" Cougar said. "Ugh! Your tongue is contaminated! Cut it off before the infection spreads!"

Panther smiled.

"The worst part," he said, "was that there was a fingernail in it. Not a fingernail clipping, but a whole fingernail. I inquired to see if this was common, and everyone said no. I took this as a sign that that whole system of machinery was breaking down, maybe fatally. But Leon said that the entropy heresy is based on the assumption that the crypt nation is sealed, its boundaries uncrossable. He said that Danielle's ascension, and our arrival, nullify the theory."

"I think it might be better if the machines did break down," Cougar grumbled.

Moments later, Jaguar returned, scowling.

"Twenty-four hours!" Jaguar said. "It takes 24 hours to form the elixir."

"That doesn't sound so bad," Danielle said. "I'll take the opportunity to relax."

"I'll perfect my skills at writing and using the transmitter," Panther said.

"I'll guard Leon and the amphibious vehicle, since no one else wants to do anything responsible," Cougar said.

"And that leaves me free to seethe with bitter impatience," Jaguar said.

He took some smoked elk from his pouch and began to chew petulantly.

17

I once saw a dragonfly stumbling in slow circles on the ground. Hoping to nurse it back to strength, I brought it home and put it on the edge of a bowl of sugar water. When I returned later in the day, I saw that the sugar water had attracted many small ants, which apparently ate the dragonfly alive. It was another misguided human intervention.

– Janet Peptide, Epistle from the Asylum

Danielle slept on the floor in a warehouse whose shelves were bare.

"Wake up," Jaguar said. "We've got problems."

"What?" Danielle said, springing into a crouch. Her bow was in her hand. "Is the elixir ready?"

"Not for fourteen more hours," Jaguar said, hastening to the street. "This isn't about the elixir. Hurry. We need your diplomatic skills before Cougar kills everyone."

"What? Why?" Danielle said. "What happened?"

"You'll see," Jaguar said.

They emerged from the warehouse to see Cougar and Panther backed against the amphibious vehicle. They had arrows ready in their bows, and they stared down a gathering crowd. Fifteen or more people brandished carving knives, scissors, bowling pins, hammers, and metal poles.

"I'm worried about them, not about us," Jaguar whispered. "Save them. I'm protecting you."

Then he vanished into shadows that Danielle did not even see. A distraught woman arrived carrying a small boy who panted frantically. Three angry men with bricks flanked her. A maintenance drone sputtered excitedly around the fringes of the crowd.

"Hello!" Danielle shouted. "Excuse me! Hey there! Hi everyone!"

Half the crowd turned their baleful stares toward Danielle.

"Could someone please explain why you're gathering around my friends in a manner than can only be described as aggressive hostility?" Danielle said.

"The food's shut off!" a man shouted. "Water too!"

"The vapors aren't coming either," said the man with the gray beard. "I need the white vapor to sleep!"

"My boy's asthmatic!" screamed the woman holding the child, whose lips and fingernails were turning blue. "He can't breathe without the orange vapor!"

"And the doors are locked!" a man said. "We can't get out of the block!"

"What does this have to do my friends?" Danielle asked, shaking her head.

"Maybe nothing," said the bearded man. He thrust his pointy scissors in the air. "Maybe it just has to do with you."

"Me?" Danielle said. "Why?"

He handed her a note.

"We found this on the food dispenser," he said.

Danielle read aloud.

"Dear citizens, with deep regret and apologies, we inform you of a temporary malfunction in your block. All food and water dispensers, vapors, and tunnel doors are affected. Regrettably, there are no medic vehicles in the block at present. The malfunction is caused by a stranger and her strange vehicle, an abomination that mocks the achievements of our forebears. In ten hours, we will arrive to confiscate this vehicle and mete justice upon its dastardly pilot. We ask for your cooperation. If you deliver her to us, the immediate restoration of your block's machinery is assured. With fondest wishes, the emissaries of the forebears."

Danielle threw the paper on the ground, and the maintenance drone inhaled it.

"That's not even subtle!" Danielle said. "Whoever wrote this obviously shut down the machinery to force you to turn me in!"

"We know that!" the bearded man said. "We're an angry mob, not a stupid one! We don't know you, we don't know why you brought this misfortune upon us, and we'll gladly sacrifice you to save ourselves. I'm hungry!"

The crowd pressed closer, and large men approached Danielle with hammers and a rope.

"What's that?" Danielle gasped in panic, pointing to the back of the mob.

In the moment of confusion, Danielle slipped unseen through the crowd to reappear between Cougar and Panther. A man swung at Cougar with a brick, and Cougar kicked out his teeth. Danielle dodged a hurled mallet. Three men with knives rushed Panther. He spun one of the men over his shoulder, into the other two, and they toppled back into the mob.

"Drop your weapons, or you all die!" Cougar roared.

"Cougar! We can't kill them all!" Danielle said.

"Perhaps we shouldn't," Cougar said, "though we certainly can!"

"Wait!" Danielle shouted. "I have food! Better than anything you've ever tasted!"

She opened a pouch full of smoked elk. The crowd paused, and the bearded man elbowed his way to the front of the crowd. He snatched the pouch from Danielle. The mob gaped as he examined a strip of elk, sniffed it, and licked it. He threw the whole pouch on the ground. The maintenance drone slurped it empty and then ingested the pouch itself.

"That's not food!" he yelled. "She's trying to poison us!"

Danielle, Panther, and Cougar pulled back their bowstrings as the crowd rushed them.

"Fire on my command!" Cougar said, eyes widening.

"Stop!" Angela said, stepping out of the crowd. "I can cure the boy. We don't need machines. We're better off without them."

The mob's murderous impulse again dissolved into confusion and curiosity. They watched as Angela inserted pins in the asthmatic boy's wrists and shoulders. He inhaled deeply, shuddering as he inhaled even more. His chest swelled. Then he sighed and began a series of slow, even breaths. Angela put her hand on his pulse.

"He is young, and his energy is strong," Angela said. "This cure is permanent. He will never need orange vapors again."

"What about food?" a man cried menacingly. "And water? We can't eat pins."

"There's plenty of water in this vehicle,"

Panther said. "And give our food another try. It's good, really. See?"

He dropped a handful of pine needles in his mouth and then passed a pouch to the crowd.

"Pine needles, brother?" Cougar said. "Seriously? That's all you brought to sustain you on a harrowing mission in the underworld?"

"Give out your smoked elk," Danielle hissed to Cougar. "We need to placate the crowd. We can fast until the warden comes for me, and then we'll easily defeat him and go home."

Cougar grunted irritably but handed his food pouch to a stooped, skinny man with a bowling pin.

"Well done, all of you," Jaguar said.

"I can't believe they didn't see you," Cougar said with disgust. "You weren't even trying to hide anymore."

Jaguar shrugged.

"I save my energy for when it's needed," Jaguar said.

He narrowed his eyes. Cougar returned his stare and then nodded.

"To the food dispenser," Cougar said.

Leaving Danielle and Panther with the contentedly munching crowd, Jaguar and Cougar ran toward the restaurant where the note was found.

"So many tracks!" Jaguar snarled when they arrived. "The mob was here. Too many tracks to sort through!"

"Not for me," Cougar said. "The man who left the note went this way!"

They ran past several streets and entered a small library. They went up a flight of stairs and found a man with large ears. He sat reading at a long table. A stack of books was at the opposite end of the table.

"That's him!" Cougar said.

Cougar threw the man across the table and into the stacks of books. The man rolled, screaming, onto the floor.

"Who else in this block conspires with the warden?" Cougar said. "How many will arrive with him?"

"I don't know!" the man screamed. "I never even heard of him until about an hour ago! He called me over to his taxi. He gave me the note and told me where to put it. That's all I know! That's all I know!"

"That doesn't make any sense!" Cougar said. "How did he know we were here? Did you tip him off!"

"No!" the man said. "I told you, he came to me! He already knew you were here! I don't know how!"

"Why did he choose you?" Cougar said. "And why did you agree to help him?"

"On account of my big ears!" the man said. "He asked me if women liked my big ears, and I said, no, sir, they sure don't. He promised me women if I helped him just this once. He showed them to me. So beautiful! Normally, they would not even talk to me, on account of my big ears!"

"Perhaps you'd like me to trim them down for you?" Cougar snarled, pressing forward with his knife.

The man clamped his hands over his ears and sobbed, rocking back and forth.

"Enough, Cougar," Jaguar said. "Nobody likes unnecessary cruelty, remember? He obviously knows nothing. I only wish I knew how the warden knows we're here. There may be other unpleasant surprises."

Cougar stared at his knife.

"Yes, brother," he said. "I'm afraid that unpleasant surprises await us all."

18

On Saturday afternoon, the sidewalk was filled
with protestors carrying picket signs. I studiously
avoided reading any of their signs, thereby denying
them the victory of spreading their message.
Before finally surrendering to riot police, one
woman was struck by 27 rubber bullets, clubbed
across the mouth and ears 13 times with a
nightstick, doused with pepper spray seven times
in the face, and catapulted across the street by a
gushing fire hose.

As she was dragged away in handcuffs, she turned
her blackened eyes toward me and opened her
bleeding mouth to say, "When you allow virtuous
actions to spring effortlessly from your heart, you

feel nothing but peace and joy, in spite of any
outward signs of struggle and sacrifice."
– Janet Peptide, The Harder I Try, the Harder I Fail

Danielle and the three brothers lay in wait in the empty room above the abandoned warehouse. She peered through a gauzy curtain out the window. The amphibious vehicle, only half full of water, sat by the tunnel door. The street was otherwise deserted.

"You're sure no one knows we're here?" Danielle asked.

"Positive," Jaguar said. "No one saw us enter, and I concealed the door to the stairway. The only recent tracks in this building are ours. I don't think anyone else has been on this level for at least five years. Just in case anyone comes after us, I set a whole series of traps along the stairs."

"And, presumably, everyone is hiding because they don't want to face the warden's wrath when he sees that I'm not there?" Danielle said.

"Presumably," Jaguar said.

"So it should be a simple matter to kill the warden and his retinue," Cougar said. "Then we give his transmitter to Leon, who can use it to reverse the commands blocking the machinery."

"I wish Leon didn't have to get involved," Danielle said. "We still have to wait four hours for the elixir. We mustn't endanger the elixir or Leon."

"The tunnel door is opening!" Panther hissed.

They readied arrows on their bowstrings and crouched behind the curtain. Two taxis emerged from the tunnel, and the door shut behind them.

The warden and three men holding guns stepped out of the first taxi. The warden wore a fuzzy blue bathrobe and slippers.

"Very good!" he shouted to the empty street. "You've left the blasphemous vehicle for us. But where is the insurrectionist? Where is the traitor to our forebears? Where is Danielle Gasket?"

His voice rang through the empty street.

"Do we kill them yet?" Cougar whispered.

"Wait to see how many are in the second taxi," Jaguar answered. "If they are few enough, we can lure them into my non-lethal traps."

"Nothing's ever easy," the warden sighed. "So difficult is this life. Difficult. But even our enemies have weaknesses. Even villains have a softness in their hearts. I was amazed when first I learned that villains' hearts contain more than barbed wire and ice. Villains, it turns out, have a weakness for other villains."

Two more gunmen stepped out of the second taxi. A final gunman roughly shoved a thin man out of the taxi. He staggered and stood unsteadily. He had long, black dreadlocks and a gray goatee. All six gunmen aimed their guns at him.

"Tommy Farad!" Danielle gasped.

"You know him?" Cougar said, glaring at her.

"I have to turn myself in!" Danielle whispered. "We can kill four of the gunmen before they react, but the other two will kill Tommy!"

"Don't be a fool!" Cougar said. "Your enemy is here, in our grasp! We can end his wicked reign! One small sacrifice, and he'll never be able to terrorize anyone again!"

"Listen," Danielle said. "You can tracks vehicles through the tunnels, right? Come rescue me. It will be easy. The warden has no idea of your tracking abilities. He'll never expect it."

"You could be dead by the time we get there!" Cougar said.

"I'll convince him that he needs me if he wants to ascend," Danielle said. "I won't even have to lie. The warriors of the free nation will kill him unless I'm there as his advocate."

She squeezed Cougar's shoulder.

"Rescue me," she said.

She dashed down the stairs, avoiding nearly invisible tripwires. She ran into the street.

"Sorry I'm late!" Danielle said. "Must've overslept."

The warden's droopy lips parted and then curled into a ghastly smile.

"Danielle Gasket!" he exclaimed. "Now bald! An ingenious disguise. I never would have seen through that."

"It might be time for you to think about a change, yourself," Danielle said. "Is that the same bathrobe you were wearing a year ago? Have you even washed that thing?"

The warden scowled.

"Stop hectoring me," he said. "It's not nice."

"And you're the reigning expert on 'nice,'" Danielle said.

The warden stomped his slipper.

"This isn't a battle of wits," he said. "This is a battle of lethal capabilities, and you've lost! But because I'm known for my generosity, I'll offer you a deal. Store up your insults in silence. Then, just before I kill you, I'll give you five minutes to insult me to your heart's content."

"Better make it ten minutes," Danielle said. "This will be the comic-insult extravaganza of a lifetime."

The warden grimaced and gestured at the gunmen. Three gunmen squeezed into a taxi with Danielle, while Tommy and the other three gunmen got in the second taxi. The warden waded into the aquatic vehicle. He tapped the buttons on his transmitter.

"Everything is back to normal in this block!" the warden shouted. "Your liberation is now complete!"

The hatch closed, and the three vehicles drove into the tunnel.

19

People think karma is about reward and punishment. It may seem that way, but really it's about the energy field trying to give people what they apparently want. When you do something deliberately, it sets up a resonance in your energy field with that sort of experience. It magnetizes similar experiences in your direction. It has nothing to do with reward or punishment in the sense of being judged. It's just about resonances that you have accumulated. You can dissolve any of your acquired resonances as you wish.
– Janet Peptide, Epistle from the Asylum

Jaguar, Cougar, and Panther held torches of burning rags. They ran through the tunnel.

"Tracks of so many taxis!" Jaguar said. "There must be thousands!"

"Ignore the taxis," Cougar said. "The amphibious vehicle has a unique tread."

They ran up ramps and down, along steep ascents and gentle plateaus. When they heard a vehicle approaching, they dropped their torches and hid in the shadows until it passed. After a few hours, Cougar halted in front of a door.

"Here it entered," he said.

Panther called a taxi. The door opened, and the taxi entered the block. A crowd watched a woman standing on her head and juggling with her feet. The three brothers slipped unnoticed to the left. They crossed three streets, turned to the left, and paused at a bend to the right. They stared at the ground and listened. The street here was empty. Squatting, Cougar pointed at the ground.

"The vehicle continued around the bend," he whispered. "The tracks here are few, and mostly of the same people. I hear several voices in the distance. These are probably the warden's guards. Any bullets fired, even if they miss, will alert all our adversaries. To avoid endangering Danielle, they must not know we are here."

"We could send an empty vehicle down the street to attract their attention," Jaguar said. "Then we can approach unnoticed."

Panther frowned.

"Too risky," he said. "Empty vehicles do not

approach people for no reason. Suspicious, the gunmen may fire upon it. They do not know about me; they apparently only knew of Danielle. I can approach as an innocent explorer while you advance in stealth."

Cougar and Jaguar nodded. Panther ambled around the bend, whistling softly. At the far end of a long, empty street, six gunmen guarded a wide door. They straightened when they noticed Panther, but they did not raise their guns. When Panther came within twenty paces, one of the guards gestured with his gun.

"Turn back," he said. "No one passes through this door."

"I don't want to go through the door," Panther said, continuing to approach. "I want to sing for you. I performed to a large and appreciative crowd around the bend. One of the spectators lamented that you six were unable to hear it. Do you have a favorite song?"

The gunmen looked at one another uncertainly.

"I like the troubadour ballads," one of them said.

"An excellent choice!" Panther exclaimed.

Jaguar and Cougar leapt from the shadows and each grabbed two gunmen's forearms, squeezing the tendons so that pulling a trigger was impossible. Panther simultaneously seized the two remaining gunmen. The gunmen then lost consciousness due to a variety of chokeholds and blows to the head.

Cougar approached the door and listened. He pressed the door, but it would not open.

"Can you open this with your transmitter?" he asked Panther.

Panther held his transmitter but shook his head.

"The door is unmarked," he said.

Cougar grumbled and squatted near the ground.

"There are two other groups of six gunmen who regularly stand guard here," Cougar said, pointing at nearly invisible scuffmarks. "One group is away, possibly on break. The other group is on the other side of this door. If I'm timing this correctly, the groups work in eight-hour shifts. In three hours, the group that's inside will come out to relieve this group. Then this group goes on break. At the same time, the group currently on break will arrive to guard the interior."

Jaguar rubbed his head and coughed softly.

"Three more hours of waiting!" he wheezed. "I'll set traps for the six gunmen who'll be returning from break."

"I'll kill these six and hide them," Cougar said.

"No!" Panther said. "I'll bind them, put them in taxis, and instruct the taxis to circle deep in the tunnels for the next four hours. When they regain consciousness, their vocal commands to the taxis will be ignored; vocal commands are below transmitters in the hierarchy."

"Fine," Cougar sighed. "I'll prepare our assault on the six remaining gunmen."

"Cougar, come examine this track," Jaguar said.

Cougar darted toward Jaguar.

"No, wait!" Jaguar said. "Oh, you're right on top of it."

"No matter," Cougar said. "I can still see it. It's an old track, five days at least. Merely one of the gunmen."

Jaguar frowned.

"Even with the air so still? Weathering so minimal?" he said. "I would have dated it to one or two days, at most."

Cougar shrugged.

"Perhaps I misread it," Cougar said. "No matter. Why does it trouble you, brother?"

"I don't know," Jaguar said. "I thought it looked familiar."

He stared long at the ground.

Three hours later, the door opened, and six gunmen stepped out.

"Hey, where's the other shift?" one of them asked. "Did Wardy tell them to go?"

Jaguar, Cougar, and Panther dropped down from ropes, disarmed the gunmen, and knocked them out. Other than a single, soft grunt, the operation was completed in silence.

Cougar bent near the ground, eyes fierce, staring in through the door. Several portraits and sculptures adorned the opposite wall. A hand-woven carpet of soft greens and purples lay on the floor. Nearly inaudibly over the pervasive hissing from vents, Cougar made the call of the red-striped frog. In response came the cry of the starling. Cougar grinned and bounded silently into the room.

Danielle and Tommy sat on plush chairs around a wrought-iron table. Danielle leapt up and tackled Cougar, almost to the ground.

"I knew you'd rescue me!" she said.

"Where's the warden?" Cougar asked.

"Through that door," Danielle said. "He's alone. The amphibious vehicle is locked behind a gate at the end of this hallway. Remember, the warden's transmitter is at the top of the hierarchy. Nothing can override any command that he gives."

Cougar exchanged looks with Jaguar and Panther and then knocked on the warden's door.

"Hey Wardy!" Cougar said, attempting to impersonate a gunman. "You better take a look at this."

"What is it?" the warden called. "Is it the prisoners? My enemies? Have my enemies escaped?"

"Oh, they're right here, all right," Cougar said. "But there's something you better see for yourself."

They heard a click, and the door began to open. As soon as it was ajar, Cougar launched himself into the room. He landed on top of the warden and wrested away a transmitter and gun. Cougar put these in his pouches as Jaguar seized the warden.

"Now what do we do with him?" Jaguar asked.

"Is there any question?" Cougar said. "We kill him."

The warden squirmed weakly, his mouth and eyes wide.

"Or we can take him with us on the path of ascension," Danielle said. "It's what he's struggled for all his life. Yet if we grant his dearest wish, he'll be totally dependent on us for survival."

"We'd have to monitor him constantly so that he doesn't ally with the brigands," Cougar said. "The moment we let our guard down, we're doomed. Imagine the brigand nation equipped with vehicles and guns!"

"I, who suffered the most at his hands, take responsibility for watching him," Tommy said. "I have often heard that the highest reward, in this life and the next, is earned through mercy toward those who need it. If he misbehaves in the free nation, we can kill him then."

Cougar narrowed his eyes.

"Who invited you to the free nation?" he said.

"Cougar, it's okay," Danielle said, resting her hand on Cougar's shoulder. "Without his help, I never would have ascended. Come with me to pick up the elixir. We'll ride a taxi and meet the others at the ice pool. The six of us can't all fit in the amphibious vehicle at the same time."

"No," Cougar said. "I stay with the warden. I fear that my soft-hearted brothers may be persuaded to set him free. Ride with Tommy to get the elixir."

"Oh, okay," Danielle said. "Tommy, let's go."

Tommy limped after her toward the door. Danielle frowned and started to pull a scrap of paper from her pocket.

"How'd this get in my pocket?" she asked.

"Not now, Danielle," Panther said softly.

He stared at her intensely until she shrugged and slid the paper deeper into her pocket. She and Tommy departed.

"Take us to the amphibious vehicle," Cougar snarled at the warden.

"Yes, yes, right this way," he said, straining in Jaguar's grasp.

The warden led them down a hall to a gate.

"Open," he said, and the gate opened.

The vehicle was just beyond the gate. Jaguar threw the warden into the vehicle, which was still half filled with water. The warden yelped and scrambled to sit up. The three brothers climbed in after him.

"Hatch close," Panther said, and the hatch closed.

In the small enclosure, the warden's breaths were piercing whimpers.

"The A1I block of the x = -1.00, y = 0.43, z = 1.00

precinct," Panther said.

The vehicle advanced, passing through the door and around the six unconscious gunmen. The rest of the long street was empty, and the vehicle began to accelerate.

"Halt," Cougar said.

The vehicle jolted to a standstill, far from the wall at the opposite end of the street.

"Why do we halt, brother?" Panther said.

"Listen carefully, so that we may all avoid rash decisions that we may regret," Cougar said. "This could be our only opportunity to secure the warden's compliance. The free nation may soon be besieged by two foes: an invigorated brigand nation and a sea nation of uncertain loyalties. According to Chrysalis, the representative of the sea nation is seemingly invulnerable to our weaponry. Is it a coincidence that we now have in our midst a man who can supply us with fearsome armaments? Not only guns, but perhaps even greater weapons designed and monitored in secrecy?"

"Forget it," Panther said. "You can't wield the devil's scepter without becoming the devil."

"I beg you to reconsider," Cougar said. "I have spent more time than you in the brigand nation."

"Perhaps that's the problem," Jaguar muttered.

"There I have seen the cruelty that knows no limits, the fear that knows no rest," Cougar continued. "And I have seen also the strength of their determination to rise up and conquer us. We have the chance to liberate them from their knavery. But if instead we wait to fall to their encircling spears, so much knowledge will be lost. They hardly know the art of camouflage. They can track only in sand and mud."

"And what will be lost if we adopt their expansive military tactics?" Jaguar said.

"Nothing to be mourned," Cougar said. "Despite their other shortcomings, the brigands do surpass us in their willingness to make a small sacrifice to benefit the whole."

He removed the warden's gun from his pouch and aimed it menacingly.

"So again I ask you to reconsider," Cougar growled.

"It is as I feared," Panther sighed, and he typed one command on a transmitter.

The vehicle began to accelerate forward. Cougar fired a bullet through the transmitter.

"Halt," Cougar said, but the vehicle continued to gain speed.

"You can't override a transmitter that way," Panther said. "Vocal commands are at the bottom of the hierarchy."

"But my transmitter is at the top, friend," the warden said to Cougar.

"And tell me, brother," Panther said, "where is the warden's transmitter?"

"Right here in my pouch—" Cougar said, and

then he gaped at his empty pouch.

"Or did you just shoot a bullet through it?" Panther asked.

"Nothing can override its last command!" the warden screamed. "Nothing!"

"Hatch open," Cougar said.

"It doesn't open while the vehicle's moving!" shrieked the warden.

The vehicle rapidly accelerated, hurtling eagerly toward the wall at the far end of the street. Cougar fired five bullets into the window. The last bullet cracked the window, but it did not break. The warden gibbered.

"Brothers, do you hear the gulls?" Panther said. "Do you taste the honey?"

Jaguar gulped.

"I taste it," he said, "though it's a pity I have to taste it in this stale air."

The vehicle achieved a speed never before achieved by any vehicle in the crypt nation. Cougar pounded the cracked window with his knife. The warden squealed.

"You know, brothers," Jaguar said, "I just had the most remarkable insight. There's only one thing—"

And that was when the vehicle exploded against the wall.

20

If there were no dawn, then dusk could not be.
Planets and stars would have naught to adorn.
If there were no night, then we'd never see
Dew ornamenting grasses in the morn.

There'd be no buds without avalanches
Of leaves from trees by end of November.
Though we prize blossoms heavy on branches,
Ice-crusted twigs are too to remember.

And so, perhaps, to watchers in the skies
Who delight with us in our shouts of glee,
There is beauty too in our somber cries.
Tears are our eyes' beauty our eyes can't see.

Though we love love and loathe it to perish,
Our smiles and sobs are equal to cherish.
    –Janet Peptide's Greatest Doggerel

Danielle climbed nervously up the stairs to the apartment. She knocked on the door. A stooped woman with white hair opened cautiously.

"Mom!" Danielle said. "It's me!"

"Danielle!" her mother said, her face crinkling into smiles.

They embraced, swaying, for several moments.

"I'm so sorry it's been so long," Danielle sputtered. "I've just been so busy with my, ah, needlepoint, that, I don't know, it's hard to explain–"

"Just come in, come in," her mother said. "I'm happy for you. I'm glad you found something that you like so much."

They sat on a squishy couch piled high with blankets and pillows.

"I like your new look," Danielle's mother said. "You know, when I was your age, I thought a good bit about shaving my head."

"Did you do it?" Danielle said.

"Of course not. You know I have no courage. I don't know where you get it from."

"Aw, me? I'm not brave," Danielle said. "I like security. Predictability. Routine."

"Really? Good for you."

Danielle's mother leaned forward, peering through thick glasses.

"Your face seems so full," she said. "My eyes aren't so good anymore. Maybe they're playing tricks on me."

"No trick," Danielle said. "I've really gained weight. My stomach doesn't hurt anymore when I eat. I think maybe—maybe the concentration I developed through needlepoint helps clear my mind and improve my digestion."

"That may be. I always felt better after mending your clothing! You never let up, you know. You ripped the knees of your pants faster than I could mend them."

Danielle laughed.

"How's dad?" she asked.

"He can't really get out of bed anymore. I have to take care of him. That's why I can't visit you, you know. He needs the orange vapors at all times."

"Can I see him?" Danielle asked.

"Yes, he's in the bedroom. Of course. He's never really totally awake anymore. Just watch out for his vases!"

Danielle walked to the bedroom and knocked gently. The caustic orange vapors gushed past the edges of the door. Danielle entered, blinking hard against the vapors. Her father lay under several blankets, though the air was warm. His hands were clasped on his chest. His reddened eyes were half-opened, and his glasses lay unnoticed, half-buried under a pillow. His labored breaths rattled high in his throat.

"Dad?" Danielle said, placing her hand on his hands.

She thought he turned his head slightly, but she was not sure.

"Dad, this is Danielle. I just wanted say that I'm really sorry I haven't visited for so long. I wish I'd had a chance to say goodbye before you got so sick. I—I don't think I'm going to see you again. But, thank you. Thank you for making me who I am."

Danielle left the room wiping her eyes.

"The vapors sting so much," she said. "Thick clouds of that stuff."

She sat back on the couch with her mother.

"You know, Danielle," her mother said, "my favorite dress is torn. I can't find the same dress in any of the warehouses. My fingers have gotten awful shaky, and I don't think I can thread a needle any more. And that's your specialty, now! So I wonder if you could mend my dress for me."

"Oh, Mom," Danielle said. "I'd really love to. But, I promised I'd meet a friend. Remember Tommy Farad? He's actually waiting just outside for me."

"Oh, no matter. Another time then. Visit again soon."

"I really want to," Danielle said, brushing her fingers over her eyes. "It's just, there's always something to do. I don't really understand it. I don't know where the time goes."

"It's okay. I was the same way when I was your age."

"Mama," Danielle whispered, taking her mother's hands, "I never thought I would go on without you. I thought I would rest forever in your embrace. But now, full of your nourishment, I must leave you, and seek my own fortune. I take along all you have given me. I stand upon all you have taught me. My success is your success, and my failure is also your success, for you have taught me that none can escape the blessed fruition of destiny. Let my heart drum out a song of love for you, and when the drum at last goes silent, I will return to you, forever."

21

Scorching sands and stinging ice,
Blood and fear and sacrifice.
My burden shifts, my legs collapse,
My vision dims, my ankle snaps.
If it please the wrathful ghost,
I'll leap upon the rocky coast.
But if it please the seething sky,
I'll struggle more before I die.
–Janet Peptide's Greatest Doggerel

Tommy leaned over the ice pool.

"I was wrong," he said. "I won't be able to make it through this. You'll have to go on without me. I heard once that only the high heretic can survive this ice pool. I'd hoped it was a false rumor, but now I'm afraid it's true."

"It's okay," Danielle said. "I'll drag you through the water. You don't have to do anything. Angela taught me where to insert the pins, so we won't even feel the cold for the first half of the plunge."

"We can try some other time," Tommy said, "not now. I don't want the elixir to be lost because of my selfish desire to ascend. Come back for me. I'll meet you here."

"Really?" Danielle said. "Will you be safe?"

"Against all odds, I outlived the warden," Tommy smirked. "Survival gets easier now."

"Then I'll get ready," Danielle said.

She inserted pins in her hands and ears.

"It's funny how I keep coming back to this room," she said, surveying Roger's remains and the amphibious vehicle that she had sabotaged.

"You'll come back one more time," Tommy said. "In 30 days, say?"

Danielle nodded. Tommy clasped her shoulders.

"Then I'll leave you in privacy," he said. "I know clothing freezes solid in the ice pool."

"It's okay," Danielle said. "I'd prefer if you stayed."

"Not this time," Tommy said, "or I'll have to jump in the ice pool just to cool down."

"Oh! Okay. Then, goodbye," Danielle said, kissing his cheek.

Tommy left. Danielle began to sweat, and she removed the pins. She waited until her skin felt blisteringly hot. Then she lifted the small vial that Leon had given her. She poured the elixir in her mouth, the only safe vessel in which to transport the elixir through the ice pool. It tasted like water. And fungus.

She removed her clothes and dived into the water. She almost surfaced on the other side before she began to freeze. She flopped out of the pool and shivered in the darkness, struggling to breathe through her nose as she guarded the elixir in her mouth. She groped sightlessly for the waterskins. She found one, poured the water onto the floor, and spat the elixir into the waterskin. She gasped and caught her breath. Still shivering, she found her buckskin tunic and pulled it on. She strapped on the waterskins and pouches of food. She held in her hands the waterskin holding the elixir. Then she began to run through the darkness.

She dragged her fingers along the wall to avoid running into it. She began to tire, but as she drank and ate, her burdens lightened. She stopped to sleep when she needed to, but when awake, she ran. The tunnel ascended the whole way.

After about three days, she paused. The echoes of her labored breaths took on a certain fuzziness. She swung her arms about until she felt what she had feared. A fork in the tunnel.

She must have been asleep when riding past this spot in the vehicle. She did not know which way to go. One tunnel led to heaven. Did the other lead to a true hell? She shuddered.

She pressed her ear to the ground at the opening to the left. She waited. She heard nothing. She crawled to the other opening and strove to project her hearing down the tunnel. But then her teeth began to chatter. Faintly, at the very edge of perception, she heard a dull humming, as of the crypt nation's machinery. Was there a second crypt nation, as vast as the one she had left?

Her eyes widened, though she saw nothing. Something terrible was happening in this second crypt. Terrible. She sprang to her feet and ran, panicked, up the tunnel to the left. She could almost feel skeletal fingers clawing her back. She could feel moist breaths on her neck. She unstrapped and discarded all the food pouches and half the waterskins. She fled, screaming, up the tunnel.

After many hours, she felt safer. She drank deeply and rested, but only briefly. She began to regret that she would have nothing to eat until she completed her ascent. Her hunger kept her from sleeping. She kept thinking that she smelled the fresh water at the end of the tunnel, but she stumbled only into continuing darkness.

She awoke once, unable to remember having lain down to rest. She tried to remember where she was. A wooded hillside? An empty warehouse? She stood and continued to run uphill. A few hours later, she arrived at the end of the tunnel. She entered the pool, dipping her face into it and swallowing. She tasted the moss, the moonlight, and the smooth stones. Carrying only the elixir in a waterskin, she swam through the submerged tunnel.

She emerged into the lake at night. She smelled roasting fish, and her stomach leapt. But she thought it inappropriate to ask for food in the same breath that she delivered her mirthless news. She saw the flicker of a small fire on the shore, and she swam to it. She emerged, dripping, into the night.

Chrysalis looked up from the fire. Her dreadlocks brushed her shoulders.

"Where are the others?" she said.

"Panther learned to write," Danielle said. "He left me a note."

"Left?" Chrysalis said. "As in, that's all that's left?"

Danielle nodded.

"I'm sorry," Danielle said. "And even the note I had to abandon. I memorized it."

Her legs shook, and she sat. She secured the elixir on her belt.

"This was what he wrote," Danielle said. "Chrysalis and Danielle, I am sorry that I cannot see you again. It was necessary to snap a thorny vine that had taken hold of Cougar. He believed that he fathered a daughter among the brigands.

He feared that his daughter, on the strength of her bloodline, would rise up as the mightiest conqueror ever brigand-born. Often he dreamed of seeking her out and spiriting her away from her benighted people. But he fretted that she, like her mother, would deride his kindness as weakness, and his generosity as cowardice. So his dreams turned toward raising an army to rout the brigands, to defend his nation, and perhaps to impress his daughter with his valiance. So he viewed the warden not as an underworld brigand, but as a necessary ally in his military ambitions.

"Jaguar and I thought to fell him unawares, but he is too vigilant for such a scheme. He would have sensed our hostile intent. Only a self-sacrificial plan, which would never occur to him, could escape his notice.

"The elders of the cherub nation hold that we are embers fallen from the great fire in the sky. These embers crackle in our hearts as flames of love, and we die when the flames flicker out. So perhaps it is fitting that my brothers and I burned most brightly at the very end. Our smoke does not rise to the heavens, but at least it perfumes a less odious hell."

Chrysalis sat in silence beside the fire. She tended the roasting fish.

"You took longer than expected," she said. "You must hurry onward. Follow the stream to the ocean. A boatman is waiting for you. The urgency is great."

"Then you should be the one to take the elixir," Danielle said. "I've been running almost nonstop for a week. I haven't eaten in three days. I've hardly slept."

"Even in your weakened state, you are fiercer than I," Chrysalis said. "You will tire sooner, but you will force yourself to push on, longer than I could. Everyone sees it in you. That's why Cougar liked you so much. But now, go! Run! Don't walk! Don't sleep, and don't rest! Eat as you run! Do not pause until you reach the sea! If your will is strong, you may arrive after three days and three nights."

"You want me to run without rest for three days and three nights?" Danielle said. "Will I die?"

"Maybe," Chrysalis said. "People who run too far sometimes do."

"Do you want me to die?"

"No," Chrysalis said. "You're all I have left."

Her voice broke, and she fell into Danielle. They embraced and sobbed.

"Go," Chrysalis gasped. "They are waiting."

Danielle stood.

"Take the fish," Chrysalis said.

Danielle devoured it before she had gone ten paces. She bounded through the dark forest, over rocks and rivulets, tall grasses slapping her knees. The insects chirped loudly, and the stars sparkled behind the silhouettes of thick branches. She smelled the fluttery leaves, the hawk's feathers, and the mossy stones. For the first six or seven hours, she enjoyed the run.

The sun rose, and Danielle's sweat splashed onto the pine needles beside her feet. Her bones throbbed within her overheated muscles. She pushed onward, and kept pushing. In the heat of the day, her vision began to blur. It was getting hard to lift her feet high enough to avoid stumbling. She took a few quick swallows from the stream and pushed onward. Her shoulders were tired. Her neck ached. Sharp pains shot through her heels. She kept running, and the sun set. Only two more days to run.

She tried to increase her pace slightly at night so that she would be able to relax a little during the day. But after only an hour at the increased pace, she had to relent. Her legs were going numb beneath her knees. Sharp pains like pins began to pierce her chest, and she wondered if she would die even if she stopped now.

As the pains, numbness, and exhaustion intensified, Danielle began to forget who these sensations belonged to. There were splintering knee pains, but whose were they? There were eyes smarting from streams of sweat, but who was aware of this? Who was aware of the blue of the sky? Who was aware of the refreshing coolness of the stream? And who was aware of labored breaths, loud as pistons, tearing the throat? There was no sense of ownership of these sensations, just as there was no ownership of the north wind.

Danielle did not know how long she had been running, but she smelled the sea. Her vision began to blacken, though she was certain it was daytime. Her bones felt like rubber. She staggered through marsh grasses, her feet splashing in shallow water. Then she collapsed. The left side of her face hit the sand beneath the water. The water flowed into her mouth. She tasted the salt, the crab shells, the crisp grasses, the gritty sand. Her nose was above the water, just barely. She was able to breathe, though the tide was coming in. She was able to blink, but she was otherwise too exhausted to move.

She was dying, yes, but had she succeeded? Would the boatman find her and the elixir? How long would Tommy wait for her before he knew that she had died?

A large, furry fly bit her behind the earlobe. Then it bit her on the eyelid.

"Go away," Danielle tried to say. "Wait until I finish dying."

But all she could do was gurgle. The marsh water was in her throat.

A man lifted her by the shoulders.

"I heard you an hour ago," he said. "Did you know you were wailing?"

Danielle hung limp as he dragged her through the marsh and over a dune. Her heels left deep furrows in the sand. She whimpered and sighed and finally managed to speak.

"Will I die?" she whispered.

"Of course," the man said. "Just not today."

He dragged her across the beach and into the waves. Gulls cried, and Danielle panicked, remembering Panther's folktale from the cherub nation. She licked her lips and swallowed. She tasted only salt, not honey.

The man dropped Danielle into a small boat. He poured fresh water from a clay flask into her mouth.

"Rest," he said.

Danielle awoke. A man wearing a grass skirt paddled the boat through the lapping waves.

"I'm Danielle Gasket," Danielle said.

"I'm Shoal."

She tried to sit up, but she was overcome with dizziness.

"Take it slow," Shoal said.

Eventually, Danielle sat up. To the right, the sun was settling into the forest on the other side of the marsh. The water was clear, and the fish were plentiful.

"What do you have to eat?" Danielle said

"Seaweed and bitter leaves from the marsh," Shoal said.

"Is it alright with you if I catch a fish?"

"Ask the fish," Shoal said.

"I take that as a no," Danielle pouted.

She ate some seaweed and bitter leaves. Her body was very stiff, and she went back to sleep.

She awoke at night in the rain. Shoal was tying a rope around her waist.

"A big storm approaches," he said. "You need a tether to keep from falling out."

"What will keep you from falling out?" Danielle asked.

"Practice," he said.

Powerful winds bore heavy raindrops. Shoal sliced the water with his oar, choosing a course through thickets of black waves. The waves grew taller and taller, crashing against the boat and flinging Danielle from one side to the other. She clutched her tether and sat drenched in a sloshing puddle. Then she felt an ominous quiet, and she saw the tension in Shoal's arms. The ocean was drawing them in while rearing up as a 20-foot wave.

"We can't live through this!" Danielle screamed.

"We can," Shoal said.

The wave slammed into the boat, spinning it in a full circle and knocking it onto its side. Danielle was hurled out of the boat. Her tether whipped her around, smashing her face against the bottom of the boat. Water rushed into her nose, burning her nostrils and throat. Her tether tore at her abdomen, and she was hauled into the flooded boat.

Shoal thrust a wooden bucket into her hands.

"Bail out the water!" he screamed over the storm.

Danielle gasped and shoveled out water as quickly as she could. She felt as though she were trying to burrow into the crypt nation through tons of soil and rock. A number of other tall waves struck the boat, but the storm began to dissipate. Danielle heard persistent creaking that she suspected was from her own bones.

"It's okay," Shoal said.

"What's okay?" Danielle moaned, pouring water over the side.

"That's good enough. We made it. We can rest."

Danielle awoke with an aching face. One eye was swollen shut from the impact with the boat. She touched her face and felt clotted blood on her nose and lips. Shoal smiled at her.

"How do I look?" Danielle asked.

"Inquisitive," Shoal said. "Fierce. Endearingly petulant."

"How did you know someone else said that of me?" Danielle gasped.

"Ask the fish," Shoal said.

"I should know by now not to expect anyone to explain an enigma to me," Danielle sighed.

Later in the day, Danielle saw the ship of the sea nation. Colorful sails and ribbons snapped in the seaward wind.

"There she is," Shoal said. "Go to her."

Danielle saw a woman standing on the coast. Danielle dived into waters. She tasted the unseen depths, the moist sand, finely ground porpoise skulls. As she neared the shore, she saw that the other woman was walking towards her. Danielle stood, and the waves rode up and down their thighs.

"Hail, crypt-born," the woman said.

"Hail, sea-born," Danielle said. "Here's the elixir. I hope it's what you wanted."

She handed the elixir to the other woman.

"The waters are the source of life," the woman said. "Yet they can be corrupted into vaults of death. Our forebears turned to the ocean to rinse away their unclean deeds. And their stains seemed to vanish into the sunless depths. But there in the blackness looms an indelible ledger of all villainy and valor, for nothing is ever erased.

"You have done well, high heretic. I have watched from afar. Many times you came closer than you know to failure. In your success, you have accumulated great knowledge of the worlds above and below. And yet, there is a heresy that even you do not know of.

"In every human heart, valor and villainy vie for dominance. The philodendrist knew this. She knew that the elixir would spoil in a crypt nation dominated by villainy. So she established two crypt nations, knowing that if villainy triumphed in one, then valor would be ascendant in the other. The nation of valor has sent us this elixir. But from the nation of villainy, bitter venom will flow. In one year's time, you will see. Prepare well, high heretic. Your greatest challenges lie ahead."

22

*Tell me, what's at the
Other end of the rainbow?
Asked the pot of gold.*
–Janet Peptide's Greatest Doggerel

"Here it is," Danielle said. "Feel this?"

She guided Tommy's hands in the darkness.

"The tunnel splits," he said. "So the duplicity heresy is true."

"You knew about this?" Danielle said. "Who are you?"

"One who serves," Tommy said. "One who expects no recognition, and rarely receives it."

"Even in the dark," Danielle sighed, "it seems that I must be wearing a sign that says, 'I like it when people speak to me in impenetrable riddles.'"

Tommy laughed.

"You know," he said, "there's a whole other crypt nation to explore. You want to go there now?"

"Not now," Danielle said. "Preferably not ever. After all the perils we survived, haven't we earned a little comfort? A little ease? With the fates of worlds no longer weighing on our shoulders?"

"What then would you do with yourself?" Tommy said. "Needlepoint?"

"Now that you put it that way," Danielle said, "I think I'll go with the perils and the fates of worlds. After a brief rest, of course."

"Of course," Tommy said.

They walked into the darkness of an uncertain future. Though occasionally they stumbled, they stumbled together.

Author's note

Baba Rampuri wrote, "Storytelling is a boat crossing time with a payload of knowledge as colossal as the ocean of story itself." Let us, then, splash deep into this ocean.

In college, I took a course in fiction writing. I hardly knew most of the other students. We didn't even say hello. But by reading their stories, I felt that I knew them more deeply than I knew some of my closest friends. In everyday interactions, I communicated at a superficial level, while the depths remained concealed. The fiction course inverted this pattern, circumventing the surfaces to communicate from the depths.

Science fiction and fantasy are called "genre fiction." People who say this seem to use "genre" as a euphemism for "bad." The genres are outcasts who eke out a dismal existence at the woeful fringes of true literature. May I invert this description of genre fiction?

Science fiction is the unified field of everything that can be imagined. Realistic fiction is the tiny subset, the minuscule niche, fenced in by self-imposed limitations. As Asimov wrote, science fiction is the scouting of the future. The scouts report back with warnings of perils, and guidance towards opportunities. What could be more important?

Fantasy is mythology. The characters are archetypes who teach us about the collective human consciousness and our own souls. What could be more enriching?

When we read "unrealistic" fiction, we let down our defenses. We don't have to justify our values and opinions while traversing worlds that don't exist. Instead, we can appreciate the song of another human soul. Wouldn't it be nice if political debates engendered mutual appreciation of everyone's unique soul song? One of my favorite novels is *Atlas Shrugged*, even though it espouses the exact opposite of almost everything I believe. I can still appreciate Ayn Rand's meticulous engineering of every detail to advance her political agenda.

I, too, had an agenda when I wrote my novels. I believe that the natural world is the temple of Creation. I believe that conservation is a form of worship, and I believe it is our birthright to reestablish Heaven on Earth. I believe this great work requires divine intervention—including the divine transformation of our minds, hearts, and actions. I wrote the novels as a prayer for the preservation and resurrection of the temples of Creation.

I'll see you in the colossal ocean of story. Stay drenched.

About the Author

Jed Brody is a Senior Lecturer in Physics. His short fiction has appeared in *Creative Loafing* and an anthology of *Science Fiction by Scientists*. His essays have appeared in *Physics Today, the Philadelphia Inquirer,* and *One Hand Does Not Catch a Buffalo: 50 Years of Amazing Peace Corps Stories: Volume One: Africa*.

He was a Peace Corps volunteer in Benin, West Africa, where he taught high school physics and chemistry. He studied solar electricity at Georgia Tech. As a member of a US-Tibet Science Initiative, he traveled to India five times to teach physics to Tibetan monks and nuns.

He enjoys yoga, qigong, birdwatching, swimming, and reading, but usually not all at the same time.

Are you a changemaker?

Stories about our world, and our relationship with nature, have been communicated among wise souls and changemakers for countless generations.

People willing to courageously make a difference in the world have gathered around campfires and sat under the limbs of mighty trees to be nurtured by this wisdom. Story is how humanity has always shared moral tales, empowered itself with knowledge, and paid hope forward into the future.

Our authors embody this spirit. They write with reverence, courage, and inspiration about the places, plants and animals, habitats and ecosystems, of our shared home—*Earth*.

In our new online place—*The Gathering*—you can connect directly with our brave authors and other bold thinkers to unshackle creative action. We all hold the power to make positive change. We just need a safe space to soar like feathers in the wind.

To connect with brave authors, like Jed Brody, join *The Gathering* now.

www.stormbirdpress.com

Stormbird Press is a proud signatory to the **United Nations SDG Publishers Compact**. At the time of publishing this title, our focus in on contributions to *SDG 13: Climate Action, SDG 14: Life Below Water, SDG 15: Life on Land,* and *SDG 16: Peace, Justice and Strong Institutions.*

www.ingramcontent.com/pod-product-compliance
Lightning Source LLC
Chambersburg PA
CBHW031953010726
47493CB00007B/2190